SAFETY CATCH

A body lay on its back half under the left-hand table. The dead man had been blond, about thirty-five, with an athletic build. He had a handsome face rather marred by the powder-burned hole in his right temple. His left profile was less attractive; there was a huge, gaping, messy hole in the cheek where the bullet had come out.

A German World War II P38 automatic lay near the corpse's right hand.

Flat-nosed lead bullet, Corrigan decided when he saw the size of the exit hole in the man's left cheek. Maybe even a dumdum. He must have wanted to die in the worst way.

As Corrigan stooped beside the body, Officer Maloney said, "His name's Brian Frank, captain. He was a CPA here. That's his desk he's lying under."

Corrigan transferred his attention to the weapon.

"Well, well," he said after a moment. "Ever hear of a suicide setting the safety after blowing his brains out?"

ELLERY QUEEN
WHAT'S IN THE DARK?

ZEBRA BOOKS
KENSINGTON PUBLISHING CORP.

No character in this story is intended to represent
any actual person; all incidents of the story are
entirely fictional in nature.

ZEBRA BOOKS

are published by

Kensington Publishing Corp.
475 Park Avenue South
New York, NY 10016

First printing: August 1985

Printed in the United States of America

1.

Everything young Miss Graves did was notable—
to males, at least. The way she finished typing the
last column of figures and drew the four copies
from her typewriter and separated them from the
carbons, for instance, was by consensus of the
otherwise male personnel of the Burns Accounting Company an artistic achievement—poetry in
motion. The way she walked through the open
doorway behind her reception-room desk into the
long bare accountants' office and laid the sheets on
one of the two working tables was a masterful
extension thereof, and it was given its due
appreciation by the two accountants.

Brian Frank bore witness with lingering candor.
He happened to be a bachelor, but that had
nothing to do with it. Gil Stoner, the other
accountant, had a wife, but the only difference
between his appreciation of Miss Graves and

5

Frank's was a matter of degree. Stoner's was more furtive.

The two men were working at different tables; their chairs stood back to back. Each swiveled as Sybil Graves came in; each could have touched her as she stood between the two tables. Neither did. Miss Graves had made her untouchability very clear at an early date in her employment.

"It's four-thirty, Brian," Miss Graves said. She had a cool, clear voice, on the husky side; it seemed made for moonlight. She also had Irish-blue eyes and a turned up Irish nose and a bust development that knew no national boundaries. It was this pectoral attribute that, above all, fascinated Mr. Frank; he indulged his habit now of beginning his inventory of her with her chest, as if he could never get enough of committing it to memory. Mr. Stoner, at the other table, rather avoided it, but not, one felt, from choice. In the short time she had worked for the Burns Accounting Company Miss Graves had become conscious of her bosom for the first time in her twenty-eight years, all because of Accountant Frank's stare.

There was nothing suggestive about it; it was too Frank, as it were, to be considered a leer. The stare had the quality of an X-ray, to which all things are visible. Mr. Frank, one felt, was a scientist of sex who was engaged in perpetual research, doing the same experiment over and over with different laboratory specimens. Sybil had been working at Burns Accounting long enough to hear the twenty-first-floor gossip. There were

6

three firms on the twenty-first floor, and Frank reputedly was the wolf of two of them. The secretary preceding Sybil at Burns had quit because of him, apparently to repair the fracture of her heart. At least two of the girls in the Adams Advertising Agency across the hall were supposed to be dangling from his belt, and only yesterday there had been something about Frank's involvement with the wife of the very man whose back reproached him for eight hours every working day.

"Two more pages will finish the job, Sybil," Brian Frank said. He was thirty-five, with a gymnasium build, Nordic features, wavy golden hair, and a long green glance, like a running sea. Out of my league, Sybil thought. And a good thing, too. "I'd like to wind it up tonight."

Gil Stoner creaked his chair about unwillingly and glanced at the wall clock. "Cheese, it is four-thirty. I got to go." He rose and lumbered over to the wall lockers and opened one of them and took out his topcoat and Tyrolean hat. He was fortyish, balding, with a thickening waistline and rather gross features. Remembering the mess about Stoner's wife and Brian Frank, Sybil felt sorry for him.

Frank made a final notation on a sheet of ruled paper and handed the paper to Sybil. "By the time you type this I'll have the last sheet for you. It'll run only about a third of a page. D'ye mind?"

"I'm not paid to mind," Sybil said. He looked at her curiously, smiled, and took another X-ray picture of her chest.

Stoner had put on his coat and hat and moved past Sybil to the reception-room door. "Night, Sybil."

"Good night, Gil."

Stoner did not glance at Frank or bid him good night or even nod. How could he continue to work in the same room as Frank, hating him as he did? Sybil wondered. Of course this was only the second day since their falling out. Maybe in time it would all blow over. Sybil ferverntly hoped so. She was sunny by disposition, and it depressed her to have to work in an atmosphere of hostility.

She followed the cuckolded accountant into the other office, carefully shutting the door. The clatter of her typewriter and the ringing of the phone disturbed the accountants, and old Mr. Burns had told her on her first day that the cardinal sin of a stenographer was failure to close the door.

Gil Stoner left without another word. Sybil sandwiched carbon paper among three flimsies and a sheet of bond and ran the sheaf into her typewriter.

4:40 P.M.

Sybil had just finished when Brian Frank came out of the other room and handed her another lined sheet.

"Winds it up, doll," he said. "What's Griswald Jewelers' number again?"

Sybil ran her index finger along a chart pasted to

8

the top of her desk, dialed a number, and handed the phone to him. She got busy on the last sheet of Frank's report, wishing he would not stand so close.

But Frank was all business. "Howie? Just finished your annual audit. Sybil Graves is typing the last page now. Mr. Griswald still there? Well, you want to pick it up so he can see it first thing in the morning? You don't shut up shop for another half-hour. Okay, I'll wait for you here."

He hung up. "Howie Craft is coming over to pick up their copies. So when you finish, you will staple covers on 'em and label each one? Man, what a pair!"

"What?" Sybil said.

"You ought to be in *Playboy*," Frank said with a grin.

"Go away," Sybil said. "Or I'll have to stop and take a bath."

"That," said Frank, "would be worth watching."

"I'm not surprised," Sybil said. "You probably specialize in peepholes."

"Touch-ee," he said with another grin. He went over to the mirror above the file cabinets and began to admire his golden hair.

Griswald Jewelers occupied the same side of the twenty-first floor as Burns Accounting, with the elevator shaft between. Sybil was typing the last of the gummed labels when Howie Craft slunk in.

Young Craft always slunk; he had a wary eye in his faintly alarmed face that came of dodging verbal blows. He was Everett Griswald's nephew, and the assumption of his eventual inheritance of old Griswald's jewelry business hung over him like the Damoclean sword; his uncle saw to that. He was overworked and underpaid and a whipping boy for every grouchy turn of the old man's temper. At thirty, Howard Craft was still unmarried; he had never found a girl acceptable to the master of his fate. To Everett Griswald, every female professing interest in his nephew had as her real objective the contents of his display cases. Needless to say, old Griswald was not loved; and, for such is the kingdom of earth, neither was his nephew, although he came in for a lot of half-contemptuous sympathy.

Brian Frank raised his manicured hand, palm outward, in the traditional Western-hero salutation to the aborigines. "How, Howie," he said out of some obscure wit peculiar to his sense of humor. "Big Chief Griswald's brave come fetchum audit? Princess Chickchick have it ready in jig-jig time."

"It's okay, Brian." Howie Craft giggled. He had found that a giggle served in most situations, especially where the he-man of Burns Accounting was concerned. "Take your time, Miss Graves."

Sybil smiled at him, took the labels and the last set of sheets into the accountants' room, and separated the sheets, adding one to each of the four piles on the table. She stapled blue covers over each set and pasted the labels on the covers. The two men had followed her in, Brian Frank watching the curve of her blouse, Howard Craft her pert Irish face.

"All set," Sybil said. "Anything else, Brian?"

He looked her up and down. "Plenty," he said, "if you'll let me sell you."

"I'm not in the market, Mr. Frank," Sybil said, and closed the door firmly behind her.

Not for you, anyway, she thought.

4:55 P.M.

They came out of the accountants' room at five of five; apparently Frank had had to explain a number of items to the jeweler's nephew. Howie Craft was carrying three copies of the report. At the door Frank gave Craft a friendly little goose, then snapped his fingers.

"Long as you're here, Howie, how's about lugging your books back down the hall?"

Craft's face was scarlet. "I had to leave the display room unattended. Uncle Everett would roast me. I'll pick them up tomorrow morning."

He hurried out. Frank winked at Sybil and returned to his and Gil Stoner's office. He pulled the door shut.

Sybil wondered vaguely why he had done that. He couldn't possibly mean to start on another project at such a late hour, and it didn't stand to reason that he would shut himself in just to put on his hat and topcoat. Funny guy, Sybil thought, and immediately rejected the adjective; Brian Frank was anything but.

Then she forgot all about him. She had nothing further to do but wait for her boss, old Carleton Burns, to come out of his private office and tell her she could go home.

She wondered if a little ESP might do it. So she knit her pretty auburn brows and wished and wished and wished.

5:00 P.M.

The elderly president and sole owner of Burns Accounting Company came out of his office on the dot of five. He was dressed to leave. He handed Sybil the letters she had typed that afternoon, which he had apparently just got round to signing.

"I want these in the mail tonight, Miss Graves. Please drop them in the chute in time for the five-thirty pickup."

"Yes, Mr. Burns."

He started for the door, hesitated, then turned about.

"Yes, Mr. Burns?"

"I don't believe—I mean in all the rush—I've told you how pleased I am with you, Miss Graves—I mean with your work."

"Why thank you!"

He cleared his throat. "I find girls these days—ah—difficult," he said. "Not like the old days. An honest day's work for an honest day's pay. That sort of thing. If you get what I mean."

"Oh, yes, Mr. Burns."

"Well." He looked at her with evident pleasure and, to her surprise, some reluctance. "Good night, Miss Graves."

12

"Good night, Mr. Burns."

He went out fast. Why, the old goat! Sybil thought. All the time he was being the great big executive he was admiring my boobies. They're *all* goats. And she felt very much put upon, and— well, there it was—a little pleased. I wonder, she thought, if I can hit him for a raise next month.

She sealed the letters and licked some stamps and put them on the letters. Then she took her purse from the lowest drawer of her desk, rose, and went over to the locker, green-painted steel like the lockers in the accountants' room, and opened it. Her short, doubled-breasted tweed coat hung from a hook; her modish little visor hat lay on the shelf.

Sybil inspected herself in the mirror hung on the inside of the locker door, surveyed the lip situation, and decided repairs were called for. When she put her lipstick away, and as she was reaching for her coat, she glanced around at the wall clock.

The hands stood at exactly . . .

5:03 P.M.

. . . and a sharp sound exploded in the accountants' room.

It's a backfire, Sybil thought absurdly.

But what would a car be doing on the twenty-first floor of an office building?

It had to be—it was ridiculous, but what else?— a gunshot.

5:05 P.M.

In the Central Control Room of the Ontario Hydro-Electric Commission, the night supervisor was taking over from the day supervisor.

"Everything normal," the day supervisor reported. "Usual load flowing southeast. When have you been hitting the peak drain in that direction?"

"Five-twenty last night. But it gets earlier every day as the days get shorter. Probably about five-fifteen tonight."

"Well, I won't hang around that long," the day supervisor said, heading for the door. "Don't stick your finger in any empty sockets."

The relief smiled dutifully at the traditional joke. As the other man left the control room, the night man glanced over the array of automatic pens moving across the graphs, making their curved lines. To his educated eye the curves told a constantly changing story of how the electric power was flowing through the interties and along the hundreds of cables of the Canadian-U.S. Eastern power grid known as CANUSE!

The graphs showed that everything was working smoothly.

5:16 P.M.

The night supervisor had just finished another routine check of the graphs. He was about to turn away, when the moving pens suddenly came to a halt. Then they began scribbling furiously.

14

He stared at the pens in horror. For some incomprehensible reason the entire flow of electricity had reversed. Instead of the power flowing southeast to meet the peak needs at a time when street lamps were going on, subways were taking workers home, and millions of householders were switching on lights, it was draining back to the northwest, which had no use for it.

The engineer leaped. He slammed a series of switches closed and jerked others open.

But it was too late.

He knew by the wildly gyrating pens that a "split" in the system had already taken place.

Across Lake Ontario, at the Rochester Gas and Electric Corporation, an engineer had just checked a panel of dials. He glanced at a wall clock, entered the time "5:16 P.M." in his logbook, then froze with his pen poised over the page. The dials on the panel had suddenly gone crazy.

Dropping the pen, he ran to a big switch and yanked it open.

Seconds later, the meters at the 737-million-dollar Niagara Power Plant, the largest in the Western Hemisphere, went berserk. An engineer here stared bug-eyed at a bank of dials and a set of moving pens that showed power output surging from 1,500 megavolts to 2,250, then, incredibly, plummeting to zero.

5:18 P.M.

At Consolidated Edison's Energy Control Center on Manhattan's West Side, an engineer was monitoring a meter that recorded the volume of power flowing in from upstate sources. Suddenly the 300,000-kilowatt influx reversed. In seconds, one and a half million kilowatts were flowing northwest, draining New York City at the moment of its peak demand.

He began wildly to hit switches cutting Con Ed off from CANUSE.

Bride-of-a-day Mrs. Gloria Vincenza of Manhattan, aged eighteen, was worriedly mixing her first cake batter with the electric mixer she had received as a wedding gift from her Aunt Juana, when the mixer decided to stop mixing. Young Mrs. Vincenza glanced at the wall socket and saw that one of the wires had come loose from the plug.

Frowning, she took hold of the cord just behind the plug and jerked. There was a sparkly flash as the plug came out of the socket. At the same instant the ceiling light dimmed to a dull orange. The bride dropped the cord as though it had bitten her. Light surged back into the room. Her sigh of relief had hardly left her chest when the whole apartment went black.

She was facing the kitchen window. Her heart began to hammer. As far as her eye could see, there was no light anywhere.

"My God!" the bride gasped to the darkness. "What have I done?"

Commercial airline pilot Jim Korph, flying at 30,000, said into his microphone, "We are now approaching New York City, ladies and gentlemen. Directly ahead you can see the lighted torch of the Statue of Liberty."

The torch was glowing and the statue was lit up, quite as usual. But Korph suddenly became conscious of a sea of darkness around the lady. He could see the lights of Staten Island; one section of Brooklyn was lit up; there were a few illuminated bridges on the west side of Manhattan. Otherwise, all was darkness.

He attempted to raise the control tower. The radio answer was so faint it was unintelligible. Where the lights of the field should have been, there was a black nothing.

In a grim voice Korph said to his copilot, "The city must have been knocked out by an intercontinental missile. We're in World War III, Bill. See if you can raise some Jersey airport that may have escaped, so we'll have a place to set this crate down."

2.

Captain Corrigan of the Main Office Squad was hoisting an after-duty drink at Maxie's Businessmen's Bar and Grill with old buddy Chuck Baer, professionally known as a private detective, when the Great Blackout hit New York. Nothing in either man's experience, which was plenty, had prepared him for such a convulsion of civilization.

Tim Corrigan looked and moved like a classy middleweight boxer with a heavyweight's kick in either fist. He was built low to the ground and, like Antaeus, seemed to gather his strength from it. His face was a construction of overlapping planes, almost cartoonistic, an illusion that was furthered by the black patch over his left eye socket. The eye that was there was brown, steady, and usually amiable. On the occasions when it was not, the word around town was "Run for the hills."

To put the frosting on the cockeyed cake, Corrigan dressed like a Madison Avenue junior executive. He was crazy about Italian silk suits and

Sulka ties and $50 shirts, to the steady erosion of his bank account. That, and an unflaggingly virile appreciation of pretty girls, were his only indulgences. And he allowed neither to interfere with his dedication to duty, about which—as Chuck Baer often ragged him—he was as corny as a Kansas field in mid-August.

Baer was taller, broader, thicker, and uglier . . . a big man in every department. He was as strong as a weightlifter. Above the swarthy skin and heavy nose and lips and jaw he had ice-blue eyes and surprising red hair, the gift of some unknown Irishman in his mother's woodpile. He would never have been taken for a junior executive of anything; longshoreman, bouncer, truck driver would have been taken for granted. But a deeper inspection would have unearthed a certain sweetness in him; women saw it almost at once, and were drawn to him for it.

Their friendship dated to Korea, when they had both been in the OSS. A shell fragment had torn out Corrigan's left eye; it was Baer who had dragged him to an aid station. Each owed his life to the other several times over. Mustered out, Corrigan's prewar record won him his old job on the Force, eye patch and all; Chuck Baer opened a detective agency.

So here they sat, in the familiar surroundings of Maxie's, on the late afternoon of November 9th, chewing the fat about an industrial espionage job Chuck had just finished, when the lights went out.

There was nothing spectacular about it for the moment. Lights went out every now and then, here and there. It brought forth the usual raillery.

"What's the matter, Maxie?" a voice called from somewhere down the line. "Forget to pay your electric bill?"

"You've got it all wrong, pal," another voice jeered. "The lights haven't gone out. We've all gone blind from this poison Maxie calls whisky."

Everyone laughed but Maxie, who growled, "If one of you comics will light a match, I'll go find some candles."

Matches and lighters flamed along the bar. Maxie located a drawer under the black bar and fumbled around. He came up with a pair of fancy tapered red dinner-candles from some long-forgotten shindig in his "banquet room," and held them to a proffered lighter. He let some wax drip into a couple of shot glasses, fixed the candles in the glasses, left one on the bar, and took the other into his kitchen. When he came out, he had four businesslike stub candles on saucers, which he distributed along the bar at strategic intervals. Then he went hunting for his fuse box. When he came back he was looking puzzled.

"No fuses blown," Maxie said. "My guess is it's the whole block. Somebody look outside."

A customer obliged, and came running back. "Whole block hell!" he shouted. "It's the whole town, looks like! I can't see a light nowheres."

"Hey," somebody said in an alarmed voice.

"I better get home," somebody else said.

"How you gonna get home in the dark?"

"Ah, come on, fellas," some optimist piped up. "What's the hassle? It's some temporary power failure. The lights'll come back on any minute."

They crowded around Maxie's plate-glass window. Corrigan and Baer quietly went out to the sidewalk.

"What do you think, Chuck?"

"Damned if I know what to think. It's nothing trivial, Tim. Not the whole city."

Sunset had come shortly after 4:30 P.M. The moon had risen a few minutes past five, however—a nearly full moon in a cloudless sky, so that visibility was fair even without street lighting. It was helped by the beams from automobile headlights.

"It's not so bad," Chuck Baer said.

"Oh, no?" Corrigan muttered. "The traffic lights aren't working, Chuck. There's going to be hell to pay."

"My God," Baer said. "All the intersections—the subways—the bridges—the tunnels—in the rush hour!"

Traffic at the nearest intersection was at a standstill. Automobile horns were blasting away from all directions.

Baer said, "We'd better get over to that corner and try to straighten the traffic out, Tim."

Corrigan surveyed the moonlit buildings in the neighborhood, the skyscrapers silhouetted against the more distant sky. A few flickers were beginning to appear in windows as office workers found flashlights and candles. It was all rather pretty. But Corrigan found no solace in it.

"I think instead I'd better find out what's up," Corrigan said. "I'd hate to spend my last minutes on earth directing traffic."

"If the world's coming to an end," Baer said, "I'll let you know how it comes out."

Corrigan grinned. It was just like the big redhead to think of the end of the world as an experience not to be missed. He fell in at the tail end of the line of customers streaming back into Maxie's, and Baer followed him.

By the wavery light of the candles they could see Maxie unlocking the cash register with a key.

"Glad I bought this new gizmo last month," Maxie said cheerfully. "The old register wouldn't open with the electricity off. I can't ring up sales, but at least I can make change. Gentlemen, I'm back in business. What's your pleasure?"

Corrigan said, "Before you start getting rich, Maxie, hand me the bar phone."

Maxie transferred the phone from the back bar. Corrigan dialed headquarters, holding his wrist-watch up to the candlelight as he waited. It was 5:28, ten minutes since the power failed.

"Detective Bureau, please," he said when the switchboard answered.

Sweeney's crusty voice said, "Detective Bureau, Captain Sweeney."

"Tim Corrigan, Sam. What's with this blackout?"

"Oh, Tim," the night-watch commander said. "We're not sure. Con Ed tells us it's a general power failure. They don't know the cause yet."

"You mean it isn't just New York?" Corrigan was incredulous.

"Hell, no. It's apparently most of the northeast,

maybe part of Canada, too. They're going to give us the whole picture as soon as they figure it out."

"Sabotage?" It was all Corrigan could think of.

"Con Ed doesn't think so, although they admit it's only a guess. We're okay here, by the way. Our communications and operations rooms switched to emergency power thirty seconds after the blackout. The phone company's on emergency power, too, of course."

Of course, Corrigan thought, or he wouldn't be talking to Sweeney. Yet it hadn't occurred to him before. It was funny about a thing like this. It upset every built-in concept, the things people took for granted. My God, he thought. There must be thousands of people stalled in elevators.

"Any notion how long this may last?"

"Looks like a long haul, Tim. We'll be calling off-duty men back; we'll have to if they don't correct the situation soon. Where are you?"

"Bar at Tenth and Broadway."

"Better give me the number," Sweeney said. "And if you leave, phone in where I can reach you."

"Doesn't look as if I'll be going anywhere for quite a while," Corrigan said. "The street out there is a nightmare."

"From what we hear the traffic jams are all over the city. What's that number?"

Corrigan peered at the plaque over the speaker; he could not make it out. He dug out his pencil flash and read it off.

"Don't be surprised if I call you back," the watch commander said. "If I can get a line, that is.

With tens of thousands of office workers trying to call home, there's going to be one hell of a tieup in the phone system."

Corrigan hung up with a feeling of unreality. As he turned back into the malty dimness of the bar he became aware of a radio voice. Someone had produced a pocket transistor radio. The announcer's mellifluous voice held a rather scratchy note.

". . . is definitely not the result of any act of war or sabotage. A spokesman for Consolidated Edison has asked broadcasters to assure listeners that there is no cause for panic. While the exact source of the trouble has not yet been located, officials of the company believe the blackout is the result of mechanical failure of a piece of electrical transmission equipment. Information as to the extent of the blackout and the probable time it will last is not yet available. This station will remain on the air under emergency power until regular power comes back on, and we will report the situation as news comes in."

There was a deodorant commercial. The owner of the radio turned the sound down, saying, "And they want me to worry about my underarms!" Nobody laughed. A man shouldered another man aside and made for the phone booth in the rear.

Baer said, "Headquarters tell you anything that makes sense, Tim?"

Corrigan shook his head. "Guess we may as well try to straighten out that traffic mess."

But when he and Baer got to the corner they found a couple of crew-cut youths who looked like college students calmly directing traffic. Cars were still backed up for blocks in all four directions, but the jam at the intersection had been broken. Motorists were dutifully obeying the young men's signals.

"Anybody beefs about the kids of today," Chuck Baer said, "I slug. Looks as if we're not needed, Tim."

"Let's go back to Maxie's. I've got to wait for Sweeney's call."

They went back and climbed onto bar stools. There was a line now at the phone booth. "Keep this bar phone open for me, Maxie," Corrigan said. "I'm expecting a call from headquarters. Looks as if that public phone is going to be tied up for the duration."

"Say, listen," Baer said. "As long as we're stuck here, Tim, how about we put on the feedbag? If Maxie's got anything edible. How about it, Maxie?"

"You wouldn't know the difference," Maxie said.

"You cook with gas or electricity?"

"Gas."

"Then we can eat."

"Maybe you can and maybe you can't. Everything in the kitchen but the stove works on the juice. I don't know if Joe can turn out a meal or not."

"With a gas stove? Are you kidding?" Baer said. "Look, barkeep, you tell that pot wrestler back there we want a couple of medium-rare steaks!"

Suddenly everybody in the bar was hungry. Orders began flying at Maxie's head.

"All *right* already!" Maxie shouted, and fled. When he came back he said, "Okay, but plain bread instead of garlic toast, and no French fries— you'll eat home fries and like it."

Corrigan grinned. "Come next Tuesday, they'll be lapping the varnish off your bar, Maxie. Which reminds me. Two more of the same. I'm not back on duty yet."

3.

Everyone had to eat at the bar. Maxie didn't have enough candles for the tables.

It was 6:00 P.M. when Corrigan and Baer polished off their steaks and tackled Maxie's dubious coffee. By then more information about the blackout had come over the bar radio.

The cause of the blackout was still not known; its extent was. In darkness were Vermont, Connecticut, most of New York State, wedges of Massachusetts, Maine, New Hampshire, New Jersey, and Pennsylvania; and most of Ontario in Canada. The black pall lay over an area of 80,000 square miles, affecting 30,000,000 people.

Staten Island, a section of Brooklyn, the Statue of Liberty, and some tunnels and bridges on the west side of Manhattan were still beacons in the ocean of darkness; their power was drawn from a different intertie.

The announcer kept reassuring his unseen— and unseeing—audience that there was no cause for alarm. Rumors were repeated as rapidly as they surged into the radio station, ostensibly to scotch them; the announcer's tone became more ironic in direct ratio to the nightmare character of the tales. Among these were the one that a diabolical Communist had pulled the switch from New York to Canada; that generating plants had been sabotaged; that a satellite passing overhead just before the blackout had mysteriously shorted-out transmission cables; that the entire affair had been staged by some overzealous government agency to see if Americans could stand up to an air raid.

The newscaster concluded: "Spokesmen for Consolidated Edison assure this station that none of these stories has the slightest basis in fact. If the blackout lasts that long, it is further reassuring to know that there will be a bright moon all night. Moonrise was at 5:05 P.M. The moon became full only yesterday, so it is still nearly full, and the sky is clear. The weather man says we may expect what during the London blitz was called a 'bomber's moon' all night. Furthermore, five thousand off-duty police are being called back to duty, making a total of fifteen thousand bluecoats who will be available to handle emergencies."

"Bye-bye sleep," Corrigan groaned.

"You shouldn't have left word where you were," Chuck Baer said, pal to pal.

The newscaster moved on to some of the problems created by the power failure. "Six hundred and thirty subway trains are stalled in tunnels, trapping an estimated eight hundred

thousand passengers. Hundreds of stalled elevators have trapped thousands of people in dark
office buildings and apartment houses. With the
failure of the traffic lights have come the worst
traffic tieups in the city's history. To complicate
matters, drivers out of gas are finding that service
station pumps cannot operate without electricity.

"The American people are learning the hard
way, how dependent they are on electric power.
Apartment buzzers won't work, vending machines
take your money and give out nothing in return,
fire alarms are out of service. At U.N. Headquarters, speakers have no audience; P.A. systems,
earphones, tape recorders are dead as dodoes. In
millions of homes electric clocks have stopped and
people are realizing that almost none of the
household gadgets they have taken for granted all
their lives will work. Carving knives, can openers,
tooth brushes, razors, electric blankets are all
inoperable. Electric-eye garage doors won't
move. TV sets won't go on and would have no
programs to receive even if they did, because all
local TV transmissions are from the tower of the
highest buildings, which lack emergency power.

"On a more critical level, people with electric
stoves have no way to cook, homes and apartments
heated by electricity, by forced air, or by
thermostat-controlled furnaces are beginning to
feel the cold. Refrigerators and freezers are defrost-
ing. At hospitals lacking emergency power, or
having only partial emergency power, iron lungs
are being operated by hand to keep patients alive.
At this moment the basement of Bellevue Hospital

is beginning to flood because its automatic pump system is out. One of the biggest shocks to Joe Public has been the discovery that no New York City airport is equipped with emergency power; the blackout has brought them to a standstill. All out-flights have been canceled; all incoming flights have had to be routed to cities that still have power. The failure made it impossible for control towers to contact incoming planes by radio, so that pilots are having to make landing arrangements through direct radio contact with alternate fields."

The bar phone rang. Maxie handed the phone to Corrigan.

"Sam Sweeney again, Tim," the night-watch commander said. "Have you fed your face yet?"

"Just finished."

"Lucky guy, because God knows when you'll get another chance. I've got a suicide for you."

"Where?"

"At the Burns Accounting Company—Bower Building, Thirteenth and Broadway. You're only three blocks from there."

"Last time I looked, traffic was backed up as far as I could see," Corrigan objected. "I'll have to walk. What's the matter with Homicide?"

"Traffic is jammed for them, too, Tim. This squeal came in a half-hour ago. We had a radio car there within ten minutes, but no Homicide team's been able to make it. You'll have to cover till we get the streets unsnarled."

"Okay." Corrigan sighed. "What's the suite number of this Burns Accounting?"

"Twenty-one-oh-one."

Corrigan repeated it. Suddenly he said, "Hey, that means it's on the twenty-first floor!"

"You get the brass ring, Tim."

"With the elevators out, how am I supposed to get up there?"

"You climb the stairs."

"Twenty-one flights?"

"Exercise'll do you good."

Corrigan growled, "If I kept my butt in a padded desk chair like you—"

"I have no shame," Sweeney said cheerfully. "Call in when you get there."

Corrigan muttered something and hung up. Holding his watch up to the nearest candle, he made it 6:05.

Baer had been listening to the rest of the newscast. When he saw the peeve on Corrigan's face, he said, "What's up?"

"Suicide. I have to check it out. Want to come along, Chuck?"

"Might as well. If I stay here I'll wind up bombed."

He drained the last of his coffee, slid off the stool, and fished a quarter from his pocket. He looked at Corrigan expectantly. Corrigan produced a dime.

"Your turn to match, sucker." Baer flipped his coin and slapped it on the bar.

Corrigan followed suit with his dime. They uncovered together. Both coins showed tails.

The redhead whined, "I'm going to start listing you on my income tax as a dependent. How much, Maxie?"

31

He paid the tab and they left, Corrigan feeling better.

Outside, the two college students were still directing traffic. Cars were crawling through the intersection now, but traffic was still backed up for blocks in all directions.

Baer glowered at the mess.

"It's only three blocks," Corrigan said soothingly. "It's better than slogging along those damn Korean trails."

"You'll probably have me carrying you before we get fifty feet."

It was twenty past six by the time they reached the Bower Building. The moon and the headlights had made visibility fair outdoors, but the lobby of the office building was as dark as the inner chamber of an Egyptian tomb. Corrigan switched on his pencil flash, and after some well-cursed blundering about he located the door to the stairway.

As Corrigan headed for it, Baer said, "What floor's this on?"

"Oh, a few flights up," Corrigan said. "What's the matter, you chicken?"

"How few?" the big man asked suspiciously.

"Come on, Chuck. You're overweight, anyway."

"You're conning me."

"Who me?" Corrigan said innocently, and led the way.

At the fifth-floor landing Baer came to a halt. "Hold it, wise guy. How many is a few flights up?"

"I told you you were soft."

"I never claimed to be a mountain climber, old buddy. If I'd known you were out to set an altitude record, I'd have stayed in Maxie's."

"You rested enough?" Corrigan asked. "Or do you want me to rub your feet?"

"That ties it!" Baer said. "I've outloved you and outfought you and outsmarted you, and by God I can outclimb you. Get going, little man."

But at the eleventh floor Baer balked again. He sat down on the top step of the landing. "I'm not moving another inch till you tell me how many more floors."

"You're over halfway," Corrigan said encouragingly.

"Halfway!" Baer howled. "*Another* eleven flights?"

"I said over halfway."

"Look, pal, from here on up it's straight talk or I resign. Just how many more flights do we have to climb?"

"Only ten."

The private detective rose. "The hell with you, Corrigan. I'm going back to Maxie's."

"Got a flashlight?" Corrigan probed the dense blackness below with his pencil light.

"No . . ."

"Looks mighty dark down there. Good luck, friend."

"The hell with you, Baer growled, and started down the stairs.

Corrigan turned off his flash. Baer's descending footsteps stopped. A cigaret lighter flamed, sputtered, and went out.

"Bad time to run out of fluid, Chuck," Corrigan called down.

There was no answer. Groping footsteps cautiously descended, accompanied by some colorful language. Then they stopped again. Corrigan grinned and waited.

"You son of a mother-loving batch," Baer yelled from below. "Turn that damn flash back on before I break a leg!"

Corrigan said, "Oh. Sorry," and obliged. Baer said something wrathful and climbed back.

Altogether, including pauses for breath, it took them twenty minutes to climb the twenty-one flights.

When they reached the twenty-first floor landing, Baer hunkered down on the top step, gasping. Corrigan, with thirty pounds less to haul upward, merely inhaled deeply, disdaining to squat by Baer's side.

"You ready?" Corrigan asked finally.

"No!"

"It's me or the dark, Chuck," he said, and pulled open the stairway door and stepped out onto the twenty-first floor.

4.

The emergency stairway was at the front of the building, the street side, which faced south. Corrigan was standing at the head of a public hall that led to the rear in a straight line; there was a window at the north end, which he could make out because light was creeping out of open doorways on each side of the hall. The main door in the wall to his left, the west side, was exactly halfway up the hall, directly across from the bank of elevators. In this left wall were two other doors, one very near where he was standing, a closed door without an inscription, apparently a private exit from one of the offices composing the suite of which the halfway door was the main entrance. At the far end, near the window, was another closed door he suspected led to a rest room.

Along the wall to his right, the east side, about one-third and two-thirds up the hall, were entrances to two other suites; there was also a closed door immediately to his right, unmarked, which must be the private exit of one of the offices of the nearer right-hand suite; and at the far end another closed door, opposite the one at the left end, which must serve the same purpose as its across-the-hall counterpart; one must be a men's room and the other a ladies' room.

The glow from the main door on the left side was dim and flickering, obviously candlelight. The glow from the farther door on the right side was much brighter and did not flicker; Corrigan wondered if that office was equipped with emergency power.

Chuck Baer came out of the stairwell to join him, grumbling. They walked up the hall together. The first door they came to, the nearer one on the right, had a frosted glass inset which his flash told him marked the entrance to GRIS-WALD JEWELERS—*Wholesale and Retail*, along with the number 2102. They walked on.

Halfway up the hall they passed the open door on the left, the office entrance across from the elevators. Its legend said, ADAMS ADVERTIS-ING AGENCY. 2103. Apparently the Adams Advertising Agency occupied the entire left half of the floor.

Corrigan deliberately bypassed the brightly lit doorway on the right, at the farther end of the hall, to check out the two facing doors near the hall window. As he had suspected, they led to rest rooms. The one on the left was marked LADIES, the one on the right MEN.

Having satisfied himself about the general lay of the land, the MOS man went back to the brightly lit doorway, which was lettered BURNS AC-COUNTING COMPANY. 2101. But to Baer's surprise, he did not go in.

"Hey," Baer said. "Where you going? From those two cops in there, 2101, is the scene of the crime."

"I know it," Corrigan said, and kept going. "But from the peek I got into 2103, there's something going on there. Looks like a wake. The dead man'll keep."

He paused in the doorway to the Adams Advertising Agency across from the elevators, and Baer joined him, looking over Corrigan's shoulder.

It was a large office, apparently a combination reception room and workroom. Just inside the doorway to their left, a railing ran the entire depth of the room, from east to west; the rather narrow enclosure thus formed was the reception-room part of the office, with a receptionist's desk, a long green leather sofa with a cocktail table before it, and several easy chairs upholstered the same way. A hall apparently leading to private offices led from the middle of the south wall, which was covered with blowups of magazine ads the management was apparently proud of.

The greater part of the entrance office, to the right of the railing, was occupied by several desks; there were typewriter stands, a long table support-ing various business machines, a smaller table containing a hot plate with a tea kettle on it, a jar of instant coffee, a bag of sugar, a jar of cream substitute, and a mess of plastic cups; and the whole west wall was buttressed with tall banks of filing cabinets. The only illumination in the office came from a single stub of a candle burning on the receptionist's desk.

There were five women and one man in the room. The man occupied the sofa with one of the women. Another woman, with long blonde hair dangling below her shoulders, sprawled in one of the easy chairs; she had sexy legs. The other three women were sitting about the receptionist's desk.

The blonde in the easy chair said, in a voice as brassy as her hair, "You must be the detectives they said were coming over."

"Yes," Corrigan said.

"I'd hate to have to hang by my teeth until you laws made the scene. We phoned in an hour ago."

Corrigan looked the other over. Everybody seemed scared. Normal. He said, "I'll be seeing you. Don't go 'way," and he went back diagonally across the hall to 2101, Baer trailing in disgust.

This was also a combined reception room and office, although it was not as large as the one across the hall. A receptionist's desk half-faced the door at an angle, but there was no wooden railing to separate visitors from the rest of the office. Two wooden chairs against the wall just inside the door constituted the waiting area. There were no other desks. A table against the north wall held a check machine and a few other appliances; there was also a bank of filing cabinets here. An unmarked door behind the receptionist's desk led to a workroom of some sort; the door was closed. In the south wall was a door lettered CARLETON BURNS, *President*.

The bright light came from a twin-mantled Coleman gasoline lantern on the desk. It lit up the room like a 300-watt electric bulb.

A middle-aged uniformed patrolman sat behind the receptionist's desk. A younger uniformed man occupied one of the chairs against the wall.

Both men came to their feet when Corrigan and Baer entered. Corrigan knew neither of them, but the older one apparently recognized him by his eye patch. It was the only one on the force.

He saluted. "You must be Captain Corrigan."

"Uh-huh," Corrigan said.

"Officer Maloney, sir. My partner here is Officer Coats."

Corrigan nodded. "Chuck Baer," he said, jerking a thumb at the redhead. "He's a private cop along for the ride."

"You mean walk," Baer growled.

The two officers grinned.

"Where'd you get the lantern?" Corrigan asked.

The young patrolman said, "It's mine, Captain. We happened to be cruising only a few blocks from my home when the blackout started. I drove by and picked it up in case we needed it."

"Smart," Corrigan said approvingly. "Now what's the story here?"

"The victim's in there," Maloney said, pointing toward the unmarked closed door. "We ran everybody out of here to the office across the hall so evidence wouldn't be disturbed."

Corrigan looked pleased again. He slipped off his topcoat, took it over to the tableful of office machines, carefully folded it, set it down, and put his hat on top of it. Chuck Baer followed suit, but in his own way. He flung his coat onto the table from a distance of several feet and sailed his hat on top of it.

"Bring the lantern," Corrigan said, and made for the unmarked door.

Officer Coats picked up the lantern and hurried after Corrigan. Baer and Officer Maloney brought up the rear. It was a narrow room with two long tables, a single chair at each, back to back. Each table was piled with ledgers and papers; each contained an adding machine. Coats set the lantern on the floor. It was immediately evident why.

A body lay on its back half under the left-hand table. The dead man had been blond, about thirty-five, with an athletic build. He had a handsome face rather marred by the powder-burned hole in his right temple. His left profile was less attractive; there was a huge, gaping, messy hole in the cheek where the bullet had come out.

Blood, flesh, brain matter had splattered over the papers on the left side of the desk; evidently the suicide had been seated when he sent the bullet through his head. The pushed-back chair and the body's position showed that he had slid from the chair to the floor under the table. A splintery hole low in the plaster beside the door, near the floor, indicated where the bullet had come to the end of its lethal flight.

A German World War II P38 automatic lay near the corpse's right hand.

Flat-nosed lead bullet, Corrigan decided when he saw the size of the exit hole in the man's left cheek. Maybe even a dumdum. He must have wanted to die in the worst way.

As Corrigan stooped beside the body, Officer Maloney said, "His name's Brian Frank, Captain. He was a CPA here. That's his desk he's lying under."

"Know how much handling of evidence there's been?" Corrigan asked.

"They all claim none, sir. He looked so dead, they said, that nobody tried first aid or anything like that. A guy from the ad agency across the hall took charge and shooed everybody out, as I understand it."

Corrigan, through with his visual examination of the body, transferred his attention to the weapon.

"Well, well," he said.

Chuck Baer, crouched at the other side of the dead man, glanced at the P38, too. He grunted.

"Ever hear of a suicide setting the safety after blowing his brains out?" Corrigan wanted to know.

Baer pronounced a four-letter word distinctly. "Somebody got shook up and loused a rigged suicide scene. Too safety-conscious."

They rose. Corrigan said to the middle-aged officer, "This was reported as a suicide."

"It was," Maloney said; he seemed puzzled. He walked over to look down at the gun; young Coats did, too. "I see what you mean, Captain," he said nervously. "He couldn't have done that."

All Corrigan said was, "Who found the body?"

"The Burns Accounting stenographer. Name of

Sybil Graves. Everybody had gone home but her and the dead man. Only two others in the company—the boss, Carleton Burns, and another accountant. Miss Graves says the other accountant left at four-thirty, the boss at five. At three minutes after five exactly she heard a shot from in here, opened the door, and found him the way you see him."

Which left two possibilities, Corrigan thought. Either this Sybil Graves had shot Brian Frank and was attempting to pass it off as suicide, or the killer had exited by a window before she opened the door from the reception room. Could that have been done?

There were two windows, in the east and north walls. The windows were the old-fashioned over-sized type that slid up and down, with a latch between the upper and lower panes.

Corrigan went over to the east window. It was unlatched. Covering his hand with a handker-chief, he raised it from the bottom. It slid upward easily, with a minimum of noise. Leaning out, he saw a two-foot-wide stone ledge below the window that ran the length of the building.

Chuck Baer had raised the window at the rear of the room to peer out, too. "Unlocked, Tim. That ledge makes a nice catwalk. Must go all around the twenty-first floor."

"For anyone who doesn't have acrophobia," Corrigan grunted. "A killer could have come from either direction and escaped by the same route. Or maybe this steno who says she discovered the body is being cute."

"You're supposed to be an expert with the cute type," Baer jeered. "Why don't you go to work on her?"

"You're reading my mind." Corrigan picked up the Coleman and said to the two uniformed men, "You'd both better come along, unless you like sitting in the dark, because I'm taking the lantern."

"Always a taker be," Chuck Baer said to the officers. "That's the captain's motto. Remember it, and you'll be captains some day, too."

"Yes, sir," said Officer Maloney.

"No, sir," said Officer Coats. "I mean yes, sir!"

They both seemed confused by Baer's *lèse majesté*.

Corrigan merely grinned and carried the lantern back across the hall to the Adams Advertising Agency.

5.

Corrigan pushed through the gate in the railing demarcating the reception area from the outer office area and set the Coleman lantern down on the reception desk. The five people sprawled about blinked in the sudden glare after the dim flicker of the candle. Baer and the two patrolmen remained outside the railing.

The girl at the reception desk leaned forward and frugally blew out the candle. She had a round Dutch face and a Dutch bob and she was as plump and scrubbed-looking as a dairymaid in a Dutch chocolate ad.

Corrigan took swift inventory. There were a lot of potential suspects; this might be a toughie. Just sorting them out and getting some line on their characters was a man-sized job. But then he glanced out the west window and saw the dead blackness of New York, only emphasized by the barely perceived candle-ghosts of the lights that used to be, and he said to himself: I'm going to have plenty of time to get acquainted. There's a long night ahead.

"Let's get you people straight first," he said. "Which one is the steno-receptionist over at 2101—Burns Accounting? The girl who found the body."

"That's me—Captain, is it?" said a girl in one of the chairs.

"Captain Corrigan. The ugly brute beyond the railing is a private detective friend of mine, Chuck Baer; the two officers you've met. You're Sybil Graves?"

"Yes, sir."

He looked her over and reached the instant conclusion that she had had nothing to do with the murder of Brian Frank. He was astounded at himself. It was indefensible police procedure to make snap judgments of suspects. Also, he had found himself glancing at the fourth finger of her left hand and feeling a bounding relief at seeing it naked. Sometimes working wives left off their wedding rings in the office, but he had already decided that Sybil Graves was not one of them; she was unmarried, unengaged. She had a turned-up nose, merry blue eyes, a voice that was at once clear and husky, and a too-wide mouth made for laughing—Irish through and through. And a pair of proud outstanding mammae that were making Chuck Baer's two eyes bug like a toad's. Corrigan hoped that his own single eye was behaving more professionally; although from certain signs known only to himself he had reason to doubt it. What was it with him and this girl? Instant infatuation? It was too ridiculous to credit for an instant. Yet there it was. She *couldn't* have done it. Not kill. Not Irish. Not with those merry eyes and that honest mouth and that freckled pan. Corrigan, he said to himself, take yourself in hand.

"Anybody else here from Burns Accounting?" he heard himself ask.

"I'm the only one," Irish said. "Sir."

He wished she wouldn't call him sir. But he let it go.

"Then I take it the rest of you belong to this office—the Adams Ad Agency?"

"You're wrong about that," said the man on the sofa, the only male of the five. He was a thirtyish man in a neat business suit and bifocals, with a hound-dog look. "I'm Howard Craft, Captain, from 2102 across the hall—Griswald Jewelers. And this lady at my right is Miss Laverne Thomas, our secretary-bookkeeper."

"Howard Craft, Griswald Jewelers," Corrigan repeated. "Miss Laverne Thomas." Miss Laverne Thomas he had met a thousand times over in his career—a mousy fiftyish little office worker with gray hair who had probably been with her company for twenty-five years. Miss Thomas wore a pair of reading glasses on a gold chain; the glasses, being unused, rested on her bosom. "Say something, Miss Thomas."

"I beg your pardon?" Miss Thomas gasped.

"Thank you." It was always important to connect a voice with a body. This one fitted perfectly—it was as flat as her chest, with an undertone that promised sharpness if sufficiently

46

aroused. Corrigan was willing to bet that she was still a virgin.

"Then the three others of you are from the ad agency?" Corrigan said. There was a general nodding. "Let's start with you," he said to the Dutch dairymaid at the desk. "Your name is what?"

"Eva Benson," the plump girl said in a plump sort of voice. "Mrs. Eva Benson. I'm the receptionist here."

"Okay, Mrs. Benson. Now you," he said to the girl with the auburn hair sitting near Eva Benson.

"Wanda Hitchey," the girl said. She had a figure like a Rubens model, spilling out everywhere. Not bad-looking, either, if you liked hot lips and the eyes that often went with them. The type that fancied herself the reincarnation of Cleopatra. "I'm a file clerk with Adams Ad."

"All right, Miss Hitchey. How about you?" he said suddenly to the brittle blonde who had made the opening crack about hanging from her teeth. He had purposely left her for last.

"Sally Peterson," she said.

"What do you do here, Miss Peterson?"

"I'm staff artist for this creative sausage factory." Her sophisticated drawl turned ironic. "It is that, you know, Captain. We're not a run-of-the-mill ad agency."

"Oh?" Corrigan said, out of his depth.

"Our revered president, Milton J.J. Adams, known by a stroke of genius as J.J. around here, regularly lectures us on this at staff klatches. Our mission is not to peddle mouth-washes and

47

deodorants, you see, but to spread germicidal and hygienic culture—whatever that is—among the great malodorous. Our singing commercials, according to J.J., are really poems. End of characterization."

"I see," said Corrigan rather helplessly.

"There's two missing," young Patrolman Coats said suddenly. "There were two men here when Maloney and I got here, Captain, that aren't here now."

"That's right," Patrolman Maloney said worriedly. "We told them to stay put in here with the others, Captain."

"What happened to them?" Corrigan asked the blonde.

She said in her mocking, metallic voice, "They volunteered to mush into the night for some food for all of us, and more candles."

"They ought to be back any minute," the auburn-haired Cleopatra, Wanda Hitchey, said. "They've been gone a good forty-five minutes."

"Is everyone else still here who was on the floor when the shot was fired?"

The blonde said, "Tony and Jeff, Wanda, Eva and I hadn't yet left for the day—the others, I mean from this office, had."

"How about your office, Mr. Craft?" Corrigan asked the hound-dog-looking neat man on the sofa.

"My uncle Everett—that's Mr. Griswald, Captain—left at four-thirty," the jeweler said nervously. "And nobody else works at Griswald Jewelers but Laverne and me. Isn't that right,

Laverne?'' he asked, as if Corrigan was about to challenge his veracity.

The gray-haired bookkeeper said in an unexpectedly hard voice, ''That's right. That's *exactly* right,'' as if he had questioned her total at the bottom of a column of figures. Miss Thomas, Corrigan decided, had possibilities.

''And at your office, Miss Graves?'' he asked Irish. ''Were you and the dead man the only two left?''

''Yes, sir. Everybody on the floor when it happened is still here except Tony and Jeff.''

Presumably Tony and Jeff were the pair who had ventured out into the black jungle after nourishment and substitute light. Their places in the picture could wait for their return; what interested Corrigan more at the moment was Sybil Graves's easy reference to the two missing men, employees of a different firm from hers, by their first names. Apparently there was a social angle to the case; the employees of the three companies on the twenty-first floor were more or less closely known to one another.

He was also interested in the reactions of the assembled company to his eye patch. He had found that people meeting him in the course of his profession reacted roughly in one of three ways: the self-conscious made an effort to ignore it that was blatant as an out-and-out stare; the insensitive were unable to conceal their curiosity; a rare few accepted it as they accepted eyeglasses or a hearing aid. All but Sally Peterson, the Adams staff artist, and Sybil Graves were of the self-conscious type.

The blonde Peterson girl was the openly curious type. The Irish girl—he found himself delighted to note—was the only one who simply accepted the patch.

Corrigan decided to challenge the blonde.

"Who are the two missing men, Miss Peterson?"

"What do you mean who are they?" Now she was staring at the patch to annoy him. He knew why. She had caught him watching her reaction to the eye that he had left in Korea; apparently she didn't like being caught.

"Just what I say. The men you called Tony and Jeff. What are their full names?"

"Oh. Why didn't you say so? Tony Turnboldt and Jeffrey Ring."

"What are their jobs at this agency?"

"They're copywriters. They write copy for ads. Like 'Drink Milko for Your Health,' and 'Stop Smelling Up the Scene—Use No-Sweat.' Deathless prose like that." She was peeved.

Corrigan did not let his grin show. He liked to get on top of types like this.

"Miss Graves, I understand you were the first one on the scene after the shot."

"Yes, sir," Irish said. Mammae heaving like twin prows of a catamaran on a stormy sea. Oh God, Corrigan thought, I'm getting poetic. I'd better not let Chuck know; he'd throw it up to me five years from now.

"Suppose, Miss Graves, you tell me just what happened."

"How far back do you want me to go?" asked the clear yet husky voice.

This time, he thought, she had left off the sir. His grin almost showed. She'd spotted his interest. Females had a built-in radar and sonar about men. He had never decided how they did it. Also, he had better watch himself. This was a homicide and, his hunch notwithstanding, she was a suspect. Maybe the hottest.

It was going to be rough, all right.

"I want the whole picture, Miss Graves. Use your judgment about where to start."

"Suppose I start at four-thirty this afternoon?"

"Sounds like a nice time," he said, deliberately dry.

It did not throw her.

"Brian—Mr. Frank, the man who shot himself—was working on the annual audit for Griswald Jewelers. Ordinarily both accountants knock off work at four-thirty, but Brian was almost finished and wanted to wind his audit up today. Now, of course, I realize why."

Presumably she meant because he had intended to kill himself and, like so many suicides, didn't want to leave a loose end. Corrigan did not follow this up; he knew it hadn't been a suicide.

"I was typing each sheet of the report in quadruplicate as Brian finished it," Sybil Graves continued. "At four-thirty I took in the page I had just typed and announced the time. Gil Stoner, the other accountant, went home, but Brian had two more pages he wanted typed."

"So you worked overtime?"

"It wasn't overtime for me. I'm supposed to stay on until Mr. Burns, the head of the firm, tells me to go home, which is generally at five. It's only the accountants who quit at four-thirty. Mr. Burns was still in his private office, so I had to stay anyway."

"Go on."

"I finished typing the last page about a quarter of five. While I was still typing it, Brian phoned next door to tell Howie—Mr. Craft there—that the report was finished. Mr. Craft came up the hall to pick up his copies; he was in the inner office with Brian for a few minutes. He and Brian came out together at exactly five minutes to five. Brian walked Howie Craft to the hall door, then went back into his own office and shut the door."

"That's right," the jeweler said quickly. "I mean about my leaving Mr. Frank alive. I don't know anything about his suicide, anything."

Corrigan ignored him.

"How do you happen to know the times of these events so exactly, Miss Graves?"

The girl flashed him an Irish grin. "Sometimes Mr. Burns sticks his head out of his office before five and tells me I can go home. It sort of makes me a clock watcher after half-past four. Especially when I haven't anything left to do. I kept looking at the clock and hoping his door would open."

"All right," Corrigan said. He had to work at keeping an answering grin off his face. "What time did Burns actually come out of his office today?"

"At five P.M. on the dot. He handed me some letters I'd typed that he'd just got round to signing, and told me he wanted them in the mail tonight."

Her blue eyes suddenly widened. "They're still on my desk across the hall!"

Corrigan found himself soothing her. "There probably won't be any mail sorting at the post office as long as this blackout lasts, Miss Graves. So I wouldn't worry about it." He could have kicked himself.

"I suppose," she said doubtfully. "Anyway, Mr. Burns left for the day, and I got the letters ready for mailing. I was just fixing to go home—I looked at the clock one last time and saw it was three minutes past five—when I heard the shot from the accountants' office."

"Did you investigate right away?"

It was an important question, since the answer might give her away. A shot, a run over to the closed door, snatching it open—that would take a mere few seconds, hardly time enough for anyone who had fired the shot inside the accountants' office to leave the desk, cross to one of the windows, crawl out on the ledge, and shut the window and inch away from it, all before the girl got a look into the room. He found himself waiting anxiously for her answer. Would she hang herself?

To his relief she said, "Not for ages, seems like. I just stood there like a goop with my mouth open. Wondering what it was. I mean I think I knew it was a shot, but my mind rejected it. I couldn't understand why Brian Frank would be firing a gun off in there. But it was too loud to have been a backfire from the street—twenty-one stories down. After what seemed like a century I finally got up

53

the courage to open the door and look in. And there was Brian under his table . . . all, all . . ." She shuddered, something Corrigan had found people rarely did. It rings true, he said to himself; it does. And wondered why he was arguing with himself.

"I understand," he heard himself say. Trying to reassure her! Worse, he went on: "And that doesn't happen often, Miss Graves. Female explanations often go over my head."

"Thank you," Sybil Graves said in a soft voice. Now he'd done it! She was looking at him with those deep blue eyes the way a young mother looks at her baby. Brother!

Sally Peterson saved him. "Ah," the blonde said, lighting a cigaret. "Captain Corrigan is a misogynist."

"A what?" Wanda Hitchey wanted to know.

"Wrong, Miss Peterson," Corrigan said. "Women are my favorite sex, but that doesn't mean I have to understand them." He turned back to Sybil, all business now. "Okay, so you delayed for some time before you went into the other room. Can you estimate how long it was, Miss Graves?"

"As I said, it seemed like an eternity, but I suppose it wasn't more than thirty seconds."

Time enough, he thought, for whatever it was to have made his escape via the ledge.

If Sybil Graves was telling the truth, that is.

If she hadn't done it herself.

6.

Corrigan let the silence build. Suddenly he said, "This was reported as a suicide. Was it your conclusion, Miss Graves, that Brian Frank had shot himself?"

Irish shook her head. "It never even occurred to me till Tony Turnboldt pointed out why it had to be. Until then I just took it for granted that Brian had shot himself accidentally."

"Oh? Why did you think that?"

"Well, I'd seen no indication that Brian was depressed or emotionally upset, Captain. On the contrary, he'd been very cheerful only minutes before. So I assumed he'd been playing with the gun, or was about to clean it or something, and it accidentally went off."

"Why did it have to be suicide according to Tony Turnboldt? Do you recall what Turnboldt said?"

"Well, Tony said the course of the bullet was downward. So the pistol would have to have been held slightly above Brian's head, the muzzle against his temple at a downward angle, when it went off. According to Tony this was so awkward that Brian couldn't possibly have got into such a position by accident. So he could only have aimed it at his head deliberately."

Genus office detective, Corrigan thought sourly. There was one on almost every case of this sort. Still, it was curious that Turnboldt had escaped the far more logical possibility that some hand not the victim's had held the gun that fired the shot. He began to look forward to meeting the absent Turnboldt.

"You talk about the pistol, Miss Graves—I mean Brian Frank's possibly playing with it or cleaning it—as if you weren't at all surprised to find a weapon near him. Did you know that he kept an automatic in the office?"

"I don't mean that at all! It didn't occur to me it was suicide because of Brian's cheerfulness. I suppose I knew it couldn't have been murder because he was all alone in the accountants' room—I mean without thinking about it I knew— so I had to take it for granted it was an accident. Before today I had no idea Brian owned a gun or kept one in the office."

"Then you'd never seen the weapon before?"

Sybil shook her head. "He must have kept it in his locker. Gil Stoner and Brian each had a private locker."

Corrigan glanced around. "Anybody here see that pistol before?"

It seemed that nobody had. Corrigan noted that

Howard Craft and Laverne Thomas did not even murmur.

"How about you two?" he said to them.

"We didn't know about Brian's suicide till after the blackout," Craft said. "We haven't seen the gun. I never saw Brian with any gun."

"Neither did I," the spinster bookkeeper of Griswald Jewelers said.

"You may have seen it somewhere else," Corrigan said. "I'll let you both look at it later." He turned back to the Irish brunette. "What was your first reaction when you saw the body, Miss Graves?"

"My reaction?"

"Yes. How did you feel? What did you do?"

"Well, I was shocked silly—"

"Of course. But did you cry out? Scream, for instance?"

"Scream?" Sybil's silky brown brows arched. "Do women really do that when they find bodies, Captain Corrigan?"

"Some do," Corrigan said, "though I take it, from your answer, that you're not one of them. What *did* you do?"

"I ran across the hall to get help. I think I had some crazy idea of getting somebody to give Brian first aid, though I knew from the awful wound in his head and face that nothing could be done for him. It was plain panic. Jeff Ring was in here talking to Eva." She nodded toward Mrs. Benson, the plump receptionist. "Jeff and Eva ran across the hall with me to look at Brian. A few minutes later—no, a few seconds later—Tony Turnboldt came over, too. Some time after that Sally Peterson and Wanda Hitchey joined us."

Corrigan ran his eye around the silent circle. "You seem to be on a first-name basis with everyone on the floor, Miss Graves. How come?"

"What do you mean?" Sybil asked, ready to bristle.

"As a rule New Yorkers aren't all that pally. In most Manhattan office buildings the people in one office don't know even the last names of the office workers next door."

The girl tossed her Irish head. "No deep dark mystery, Captain Corrigan. Griswald Jewelers and the Adams Ad Agency are both clients of the firm I work for, Burns Accounting. For business reasons we see a lot of one another, especially being on the same floor."

"Well, now, not always for business reasons, dear," drawled the brittle blonde named Sally Peterson. "Shouldn't we make that clear to this nice pirate? There's been some interbreeding on this floor, Captain."

Corrigan saw Wanda Hitchey, the agency's sultry file clerk, frame an unladylike word with her juicy lips. Her green eyes glittered a similar message to the ad agency's blonde staff artist. He was tempted to follow up the clue, then decided to hold off. He preferred to develop evidence in some sort of orderly sequence; to be sidetracked often meant losing sight of the goal.

He said to Sybil, "You heard the shot at three minutes after five, yet the police weren't called until five-thirty. Why the delay, Miss Graves?"

"We just didn't get around to it, Captain. Tony Turnboldt kept pacing off distances and reconstructing what had happened, and that sort of a thing. By the way, nobody touched anything. Tony was insistent about us all standing well back from Brian's body, and he didn't touch Brian or the gun, either. He just squatted near it for a few seconds, and looked things over."

Corrigan was ready to loathe Mr. Turnboldt on sight. He hated amateur sleuths; they were usually the life-of-the-party type, and he had known more than one case when their eagerness to show off had messed up vital clues. At least this one had had the common sense to keep his paws off things he wasn't equipped to handle. The fact that he had missed the significance of the P38's safety being on—or hadn't noticed it at all—Corrigan could not fault him for. A veteran police officer, not to mention the youngster Coats, had missed it, too.

"This monkey business went on for almost a half-hour, Miss Graves?"

"Oh, no, in the middle of everything all the lights went out."

"That took the spotlight, you might say, away from poor Brian," Sally Peterson remarked. "And it was Tony, of course, who took charge again."

"He shooed us all out into the outer office of Burns Accounting," the auburn-haired siren of Adams Ad Agency, Wanda Hitchey, said. "We had ourselves a time crawling around looking for candles or a flashlight."

Mrs. Benson, the Adams receptionist, said, "It was Jeff Ring, the other copywriter, who finally

59

dug up a flash, Captain. And Sally—Miss Peterson—found the candle in her studio." She indicated the extinguished stub on the reception desk.

"By then something like ten or fifteen minutes had passed, Captain," the blonde artist added. "As soon as we had some light, Tony phoned the police."

"Somebody taking my name in vain?" asked a voice from the doorway.

Two men toting big paper bags stood there. Corrigan examined the speaker with interest. Tony Turnboldt was in his early thirties, suave, handsomely saturnine, tall enough to make most women have to look up to him, with a curl to his lips that gave him a permanent half-smile, not altogether pleasant. A real bearcat with the ladies, Corrigan dubbed him; no doubt considered himself God's gift to women; was a charter subscriber to *Playboy*, patterned himself after Hugh Hefner—in fact, he looked a little like Hefner. He began to understand Sally Peterson's remark about office interbreeding on the twenty-first floor. If so, Copywriter Turnboldt of Adams Ad was the chief breeder.

The co-worker with him, no doubt the copywriter named Jeff Ring, was of a different species. He was well up in his forties, with a belly he had long since given up on, a papoose face, and the makings of a double chin. His mental life was probably as libidinous as Turnboldt's, but his would be a fairly hopeless chase, with Terrible Tony as his competition.

Both men were wearing hats and topcoats. Turnboldt was carrying a flashlight; he stuffed it into his topcoat pocket at sight of the Coleman lantern.

The pair pushed through the wooden gate and dumped their bags on the desk. Only then did Turnboldt look around and give Corrigan's eye patch a cool once-over.

"Five'll get you ten you're Captain Tim Corrigan of the Main Office Squad," he said. He had a deep, carefully rehearsed masculine voice.

"You win," Corrigan said. "How did you know?"

"I'm something of a cop buff," Turnboldt said. "Recognized you by that patch you wear." He advanced with outstretched hand. "I'm Tony Turnboldt."

Corrigan touched the proffered hand and dropped it. Turnboldt immediately offered it to Chuck Baer, along with a questioning look.

"Chuck Baer," the private detective said. "I'm just a friend of Captain Law here. Ignore me."

The other copywriter introduced himself as Jeffrey Ring; he did not offer to shake hands. He seemed nervous. Both took off their coats and hats and hung them in a closet across the room.

"What did you bring us to eat?" Sally Peterson demanded.

"Chink chow," Turnboldt said, which did not endear him further to Corrigan. "Egg foo yong, chop suey, fried rice—the works."

"You ought to see those streets," Ring said. "Like it's the end of the world. If you ask me, maybe it is."

"Then let's make hay while the moon shines," Turnboldt said with a cheerful wink at the assembled females; and he began to unload the contents of the two shopping bags. There were savory-smelling cardboard buckets and cartons, paper plates, napkins, plastic utensils, two bottles of Scotch, three bottles of bourbon and one of vodka, some bottles of mix, a cellophane bag full of ice cubes, and half a dozen foot-long candles.

"Looks like you're planning a party," Sally Peterson said. "Or a wake."

"Wasn't Brian Irish?" grinned Turnboldt, to Sybil Graves.

"I didn't compare genealogies with him," the Irish girl said with a toss of her dark locks. So she didn't like Tony Turnboldt, either. Corrigan found himself pleased.

"Look, if we had to go up and down twenty-one flights of stairs, Jeff and I thought we might as well make it an occasion. Anyway, from the reports we heard, this blackout may last and last." Turnboldt glanced at Corrigan. "Any objections if we tie in to this feed, Captain? If there's one thing I hate it's Chink feed that's cold."

"Go ahead and eat," Corrigan said. "I have to call into headquarters."

"You and Mr. Baer care to join us? We bought enough for an army."

"Thanks, but we've already eaten."

"How about you flatfeet?" Turnboldt asked the two uniformed men.

They both looked at Corrigan hungrily. He

said, "Have you had your dinners?"

"No, sir," Maloney said quickly.

"Well, you probably won't get it anywhere else tonight. Go ahead." He said to the copywriter, "Better light some of those candles. I'm taking the Coleman."

Turnboldt lit three candles. He used ashtrays as holders and fixed the candles to them with melted wax. He spotted them at three different locations about the office.

Corrigan carried the lantern back across the hall to the Burns Accounting Company reception room. Chuck Baer ambled after him. Corrigan set the lantern down on Sybil Graves's desk and dialed headquarters. He got a busy signal. He tried again, with the same result. He managed to get through to a supervisor, identified himself, and explained his problem. Somehow she got him an open line. When headquarters answered, he asked for the Detective Bureau.

Sam Sweeney answered. "I'm at the Burns Accounting Company, Sam. Better get a Homicide team over here. There is no suicide. I made it murder."

"Oh?" the night-watch commander said. "Then I guess you've got yourself a murder case, Tim."

"What's that supposed to mean?" Corrigan demanded.

"There's not a chance of getting Homicide up there to cover a case already being covered. They're all out climbing stairs. I'll switch you to Homicide so you can report what you've got, but I can tell you now, you're stuck."

Corrigan growled, "Okay, Sam, switch me."

The switchboard operator came on and Captain Sweeney had Corrigan connected. Sergeant Dave Bender answered.

"Tim Corrigan, Dave. I'm over at the Bowers Building on that reported suicide."

"Oh, yeah," the Homicide officer said. "Name of Brian Frank. Sweeney tagged you, I see. What's the scoop, Tim?"

"Looks like a suicide except for one thing. The dead man set the safety on the pistol after blowing out his brains."

"One of those cute ones. Glad it's yours. And it is, boy. All yours. There's nobody here."

"I'll need some help, Dave," Corrigan said. "A lab crew, fingerprint man, photographer, M.E., not to mention a morgue bus."

"You must be kidding. Isn't that on the twenty-first floor?"

"I climbed it."

"We've already gone round and round with the lab about a couple of other cases since the blackout started. They'll drag equipment up six flights. Anything higher than that gets tabled till power comes back on. You'll have to improvise, Tim. You don't really expect the morgue boys to carry a basket down twenty-one flights, do you?"

"How about an M.E.?"

"They're too busy to go mountain climbing just to look at a stiff. Bellevue's filling up with car-accident cases and people who fell down stairs in the dark, not to mention the usual quota of baby deliveries, drunks, and the rest. And they're on only partial emergency power over there. If it was to save a life, I could maybe get you a doctor. But this guy'll be just as dead when power comes back on."

"You're a fat lot of help. Don't know why I bothered to call in."

"We're always pleased to hear from you, Captain," Bender said cheerfully. "Call back any time. Ask for anything but service."

"Dink yourself," Corrigan said, and hung up.

"Problems?" Chuck Baer asked him.

"I'm on my own," Corrigan grunted. "Supposed to improvise."

"Back to the gaslight days of Sherlock Holmes," the redhead said with a grin. "Without the gas. I've often wondered how you geniuses would make out if you were cut off from the scientific services that do your work for you. Think you can solve this one with just what's in your head, Captain? If any."

"You can go dink yourself, too." Corrigan grabbed the Coleman and made for the door.

"What about him?" Baer asked, pointing his massive thumb at the closed door of the accountants' room.

"He'll keep."

"Aren't you glad it isn't mid-August? I was thinking of those stinking Korean battlefields."

"You would," Corrigan snarled, and headed across the hall.

7.

They found their assorted suspects in the reception room of the advertising agency munching away in the candlelight as though they never expected to see food again. It's going to be interesting to see these people's habits and constraints of a lifetime crumble away bit by bit under the impact of the catastrophe, Corrigan thought. It suddenly occurred to him that the blackout might make his task easier. Unless his street knowledge of psychology was all off, he was going to be investigating an increasingly uninhibited group. The normal wariness of a killer trapped by time and place with his hunter might be compromised by a growing recklessness. It was something to keep his eye peeled for.

He set the Coleman down, and Eva Benson immediately blew out Turnboldt's candle on the reception desk.

"Little Eva's one of those folks," the blonde staff artist drawled, "who write letters to their

Congressman about conserving the California redwoods."

"Why waste anything, Sally?" the plump receptionist said. She went over to the hot plate and felt the tea kettle. "It isn't even warm yet," she said fretfully.

"It's not just the lights that are off, my dear," Sally Peterson smiled. "It's *all* the electricity. Verstand now?"

The Dutch-type girl blushed. She flicked the switch of the hot plate to OFF and returned to her desk. Tony Turnboldt unscrewed the cap of a bottle of bourbon and set the bottle before her. "Try this, honey. It'll do more for you than coffee."

"Oh . . . you," the young married woman said; but it seemed to Corrigan that she was not displeased. He wondered how long she had been married, and what the long dark night and Turnboldt's undisguised interest were going to do to her marriage vows.

Corrigan waited patiently until they were all through eating. When the cartons and paper plates had been consigned to a waste basket, he said, "We're getting back to business." He turned suddenly. "Let's start with you, Mr. Craft," he said to the timid little jeweler with the bifocals. "You heard what Miss Graves said about your coming up the hall to pick up the audit report and leaving again at five minutes to five. You verify that?"

Craft said quickly, "Yes. Yes, I do. To the dot, Captain."

Corrigan raised the brow over his good eye.

"You were clock-watching, too?"

"I always do when it's near five. We have a time vault in our office in which we put away our jewelry for the night. I have to set it at exactly five P.M. every day, so I naturally keep looking at the clock."

Corrigan thought this over. He was familiar with bank procedures, but jewelry firms didn't necessarily follow the same pattern in setting their time locks. Or did they? He decided to ask. "Do you always have somebody witness your setting the time lock, Mr. Craft?"

"Oh, yes," Howard Craft said, and Corrigan noticed that gray little Miss Thomas unconsciously nodded. "That's standard practice in the trade. Otherwise some dishonest employee could set it to open in the middle of the night and sneak back to clean out the safe. When my uncle— Mr. Griswald—is still around at five, he watches me. Today he'd gone home earlier, so Laverne— Miss Thomas—was my witness."

"You keep records of your settings?"

"Of course. That's standard, too. We have a vault logbook."

Corrigan nodded. 'Now let me get this straight. You left Brian Frank at exactly four fifty-five, Mr. Craft. This would have got you back to your own office at, say, four fifty-six, unless you stopped in at the men's room or something. Did you?"

"No, I went right back to our office, and you're right, Captain. It was exactly four fifty-six by the clock in the display room when I walked in."

Corrigan turned to little Laverne Thomas.

"You were there when Mr. Craft returned from Burns Accounting, Miss Thomas?"

"I was in my own office," the bookkeeper nodded. "That's just off the display room."

"Maybe I'd better see your place so that I thoroughly understand this. Would you both come with me, please?"

He picked up the lantern and led the way. Chuck Baer trailed the trio down and across the hall.

At the entrance to Griswald Jewelers, Howard Craft took a key from his pocket and unlocked the frosted-glass door. They all went in, Corrigan holding the lantern aloft.

The display room was no different from any ordinary jewelry store. It was perhaps thirty feet by eighteen, with glass display cases forming a counter running around three sides of the office. An electric clock on the wall above the entrance registered the time of the power failure, 5:18. The wall clock in Sybil Graves's office, also the one in the reception room of the ad agency, Corrigan recalled, registered the same time, which meant that the clocks in all three offices must have been perfectly synchronized when the power blew.

There were doors off either side of the display room. The one to the left was lettered PRIVATE, the one to the right was blank.

Laverne Thomas indicated the door to the right. "That's where I work, Captain Corrigan."

Corrigan opened the door. By the light of the lantern, he could see that it was a dingy, narrow office with a single desk, a typewriter stand, a group of filing cabinets, a work table, and a couple of extra plain chairs. There was no wall clock here. Corrigan glanced at the woman's wrist and saw that she wore a tiny watch.

He said to the young jeweler, "Okay, Mr. Craft, you entered the display room with the audit report at four fifty-six P.M. Miss Thomas was here in her office, and your uncle had gone home. What did you do during the four minutes from then until you set the time lock?"

Craft looked puzzled by the question, but he answered readily enough. "Well, first I carried the copies of the report into Uncle Everett's office and laid them on his desk." He pointed to the door to the left marked PRIVATE.

Corrigan walked over, opened this door, and held the lantern up. It was a wood-paneled office—the paneling, of walnut, looked old and neglected—with a large old-fashioned walnut desk and swivel chair dominating the room, an ancient brown leather chair and smoking stand for visitors, and nothing else except a walk-in vault. The vault occupied the narrow strip of wall on the hall side of the office; as Corrigan recalled the general layout of the floor, it must be right next to the elevator shaft. A hell of a place to put a vault, he thought. Even if the outer wall were reinforced, it gave a gang of jewel thieves an outside place to work their way in—two outside places, the public hall and the inside of the elevator shaft. They wouldn't even have to gain access to the inside of old Everett Griswald's office. Well, Corrigan thought, that's not my business.

He took the lantern over to the desk and examined the bound audit reports. They were an original and two carbon copies. A label on the cover of each announced that it was the annual audit of the books of Griswald Jewelers for the fiscal year November 1st to October 31st, prepared by Brian Frank, C.P.A., of the Burns Accounting Company.

Corrigan turned to Craft. "So you're in here, you've just laid the reports on the desk, and it's still four minutes to five. Then what?"

Again Craft looked puzzled. "I went back into the display room and rearranged some stock. That took two minutes. At two minutes of five I stuck my head in Laverne's office and told her it was time to set the vault. We came back in here together, waited until exactly five, and I set the lock in her presence."

"I'd like to see your vault log."

Craft went to Everett Griswald's desk, opened the center drawer, and took out a small cloth-bound ledger. He opened it to the page containing the last entry and handed the book to Corrigan.

The page was divided into several columns, respectively headed *Date, Time, Setting in Hours,* and *Witnessed By*. There were two sub-columns under the last heading. Opposite *November 9* had been entered 5:00 P.M., 16, and the two sets of initials H.C. and L.T.

"I always set it for sixteen hours so the vault will open at nine A.M.," Craft explained. "Except on weekends, of course, when I set it for sixty-four hours."

71

"You open at nine every morning?"

"Nine-fifteen for customers. But I come in early—I'm always the first one in—to open the vault and set out whatever pieces or lots Uncle Everett wants specially displayed that day."

Laverne Thomas said in a worried voice, "I just thought, Howie. The clock mechanism is stopped all the time the power is off."

She glanced up at the wall clock, realized it was not working, and adjusted the reading glasses hanging around her neck to her nose to peer at her watch. It was a delicate lady's wristwatch with a miniature face.

"Seven thirty-five," the bookkeeper said. "Which means the power's already been off two hours and twenty-seven minutes. Even if it went back on right now, we couldn't open the vault until after eleven tomorrow morning. What will Mr. Griswald say?"

Corrigan glanced at his own watch; its time agreed with the bookkeeper's.

Howard Craft looked distressed. "We'll have to tell customers to come back later. Uncle Everett will be fit to be tied."

"Uncle Everett may have no customers for a long time," Corrigan remarked, "vault or no vault. This is a major power failure, and there's no telling when we'll have electricity again. After you set the time lock, Mr. Craft, what did you do?"

"I don't understand what all this has to do with Brian Frank," the little jeweler said nervously. "I switched off the light in here and we both went into Laverne's office to get our coats—that's where they're kept, in a closet. I turned off Laverne's light, we both came out into the display room, and we were standing talking about something when all of a sudden the light in the display room went out. I thought at first it was some break in the fluorescents, but when we saw that the hall was dark, too, and the other two offices on the floor, we realized that something drastic had happened."

Corrigan looked at the gray-haired woman. She nodded. "That's exactly how it happened, Captain Corrigan."

Unless they were in collusion, the account gave them both perfect alibis for the time of the murder. Which was what he had been probing for. The more suspects he could eliminate, the closer he would be to Frank's killer.

He said, "According to Miss Graves, the shot was fired at exactly three minutes past five. You were getting into your coats about then. Neither of you heard a shot?"

Miss Thomas shook her head. Craft said, "The elevator shaft is between us and Burns Accounting, Captain. As I understand it, too, the door to the room where Brian Frank worked was shut and the entrance to Burns Accounting was shut; and our hall door was shut, too. We knew nothing of Brian's suicide till we'd felt our way up the hall to see if anyone knew what had happened. At that we didn't learn about Brian till after someone had found a flashlight and someone else had lit a candle."

Corrigan nodded. "One last thing, Mr. Craft. You were in Frank's office with him a mere few minutes before his death. Did he say anything unusual, act in any way out of the ordinary?"

Craft replaced the vault logbook in his uncle's drawer and shut it, shaking his head. "I was absolutely flabbergasted when I heard he'd shot himself. He'd seemed normal minutes before, even cheerful. I still can't believe it. In spite of what Tony Turnboldt says, an accident still makes more sense to me."

Corrigan did not comment. "What did you talk about those few minutes in his office?"

"The audit. He explained one or two points he wanted me to pass on to my uncle."

"Then I guess that does it. Let's go up the hall to Burns Accounting. I want both of you to look at that P38."

"P38?" Howie Craft said.

"The automatic that killed Frank."

"P38." Craft looked alarmed. "That's funny . . ."

He snatched open the bottom right-hand drawer of the desk and rummaged. Then he rapidly searched the other drawers. Corrigan and Baer watched him with mounting curiosity.

"It's gone," Craft cried. He seemed in a panic.

"What's gone, Mr. Craft?" Corrigan asked patiently.

"My uncle's P38. How do you like that? Brian swiped Uncle Everett's gun to kill himself!"

Corrigan said, "How would Frank know your uncle kept a gun in his desk? And more to the point, how would he get at it?"

Craft's timid face colored. But there was a

74

dogged something in the set of his unimpressive jaw. "My uncle is always after me about security, as if I were a watchdog or something. After all, I have to go—" he glanced at Laverne Thomas, and away, hastily—"I mean, visit the men's room sometimes to—well—wash up and things, and sometimes it's when Uncle Everett is out to lunch, or he's left early. Or it could be I have to step into Miss Thomas's office. My uncle keeps saying, 'Don't ever leave the display room unless you lock the door.' What am I supposed to do, lock it every time I have to answer a call of nature?" Corrigan could not believe his ears; he could not recall anyone ever having used that nice-nellie phrase in his hearing. Maybe I don't meet the right people, he thought. "So once in a while the display room may be unattended for two-three minutes. If my uncle was out to lunch, Brian could have slipped into this office then."

"All right," Corrigan said. "But how would Frank know your uncle kept a gun here in the first place?"

Unexpectedly, the bookkeeper answered. "Everyone on the twenty-first floor knew that, Captain Corrigan. Because of our robbery."

"You had a robbery? When?"

"Two weeks ago," Craft said. "A pair of masked bandits held me up. I was alone in the display room at the time. Right in the middle of the holdup, Uncle Everett yanked open his door and started blazing away like Billy the Kid. He shot one bandit in the gun arm and the other in the leg. Later it turned out they were carrying toy pistols, but Uncle Everett didn't know that. The whole floor flocked over to see the excitement, including Brian Frank. After the police came," Craft said bitterly, "my uncle, who's a bit of a ham—he always likes to be the center of attention—"

"And that's a fact," interjected Laverne Thomas with a grimace of her thin lips.

"—insisted on re-enacting what he kept calling 'the shootout.' If you ask me, he watched too many TV shows. His favorite is *Kojak*. Anyway, that's how Brian knew he had a gun and where he kept it."

Corrigan frowned. Why hadn't any one of the group across the hall mentioned recognizing the pistol? Or at least remarked on its similarity to the old jeweler's?

"Did your uncle have his weapon registered with the police department, Mr. Craft?"

"Sure. He has a permit to carry it, but doesn't."

Corrigan said, "Thanks, both of you. Suppose you go back and join the others." He nodded to Baer. "Come on, Chuck. I want another look at that P38."

8.

Corrigan set the Coleman lantern on the floor of the death room and stooped to read the serial number on the frame of the P38. He jotted the number in his notebook, picked up the lantern again, and went back to the outer office, where he called headquarters and asked for Gun Records.

A sergeant answered.

"This is Captain Corrigan of the Main Office Squad. I want a check on a German P38 that's supposed to be registered." He read off the serial number. After a short recess, the sergeant came back on the phone.

"It's registered to an Everett Griswald, president of Griswald Jewelers, Bower Building. He's also got a permit to carry it."

Corrigan said thanks and hung up. "It's Griswald's gun, all right, Chuck. Let's rejoin the pigeons and find out why no one's admitted to seeing it before."

It's starting, he thought, as he and Baer paused

in the Adams Advertising Agency doorway.

The table holding the hot plate had become an improvised bar. A bottle of Scotch, a bottle of bourbon, and the one bottle of vodka had been opened. Plastic cups had been pressed into service as highball glasses. The liquor bottles were beginning to show perceptible space. Everybody was laughing, and voices had a slightly hysterical pitch. It was as if there were no shattered corpse across the hall, and life in a Manhattan office building in the light of candles was one big party, an every-night occurrence.

The two officers leaning against the wall looked envious. Corrigan felt sorry for them, especially the older one, Maloney, who looked as if his feet were hurting him. He could have used a slug of bourbon himself.

This may develop into one hell of a night at that, Corrigan thought.

Tony Turnboldt, handsome copywriter and *enfant terrible* of the twenty-first floor, was switching a transistor radio from station to station, apparently in search of a dance band, but he was getting nothing but rehashes of the oddly uninformative news of the blackout. Most of the eastern seaboard seemed involved. The cause was still undetermined. Power officials were taciturn or impossible to interview. Manhattan Island was one big traffic tangle.

"Hell, we know all that," Wanda Hitchey said in an open-mouthed sort of voice. "Get some music, Tony, will you?" She was standing beside

Turnboldt, twitching her hips in an impromptu frug, or whatever it was, as she waited for Turnboldt. But Corrigan was more interested in the other copywriter, the fattening Jeff Ring. Ring was eying Sybil Graves and licking his lips. He's not licking the vodka off them, Corrigan thought. The Irish girl was ignoring him, although Corrigan knew she was entirely aware of him.

He set the lantern down on the railing. "Turn that set off, Mr. Turnboldt."

"We're just getting started, Captain," Turnboldt objected. "Haven't you ever been to an Irish wake?"

"You'll have to postpone your partying till this investigation is completed. Turn it off." The handsome copywriter shrugged and obeyed. "Now please, all of you, sit down and listen to me."

The Hitchey girl looked daggers at him. But they all sat down. Corrigan looked them over grimly.

"Captain Kidd is peeved about something," Sally Peterson said. "What did who do now, Captain?"

Corrigan let his one good eye look the blonde artist over. After a moment she glanced away.

"I'm plenty peeved," Corrigan snapped. "How come none of you recognized that P38 when you all saw it a couple of weeks ago and knew where Mr. Griswald kept it?"

Tony Turnboldt said in a surprised voice, "That was old Griswald's gun Brian used?"

"Yes."

The Cassanova of 2103 shrugged. "How would we know it was the same gun? As far as I'm concerned, I assumed it was one Brian'd been keeping in his locker. All P38s look alike, don't they?"

The man had a point.

"Just the same, one of you could have mentioned it."

Sally Peterson said, "*All* guns look alike to me. I thought a P38 was an airplane."

"You're dating yourself, darling," Wanda Hitchey giggled. "The P38 was a World War II plane."

Sally gave the sultry file clerk a killing smile. "If this was murder instead of suicide, dear, you'd never be suspected. You'd claw a man to death, not shoot him."

Corrigan wrenched the conversation back on the track. He said to Jeffery Ring, "Miss Graves says she ran across the hall after discovering the body and found you and Mrs. Benson here. Is that right?"

Ring and the plump receptionist nodded.

"How long had you two been here together?"

Ring pulled resentfully at his incipient double chin. "That sounds as though you're fishing for alibis, Captain. Why would we need alibis in a suicide case?"

Corrigan said smoothly, "I'm trying to get a complete picture of the situation on this floor at the time the gun went off, Mr. Ring. It's routine in all violent deaths—accidents, suicides, or murders. By the way, if you think your answers may tend to incriminate you, you have a constitutional right to refuse to answer."

Jeff Ring looked startled. He glanced hastily at the receptionist. "Five minutes, maybe, Eva?"

"I'd guess ten," Mrs. Benson said. "I looked at the clock just a minute or two before you came out of your office, and it was ten to five then."

If they were telling the truth, this eliminated two more suspects.

"Did either of you hear the shot?"

Both said they hadn't. The door to the hall had been shut, like the door to Griswald Jewelers. With the entrance to Burns Accounting and the door to Brian Frank's office closed, there had been three closed doors and considerable distance between the pair and the pistol shot.

"Besides, I was laughing too loud to have heard anything," Eva Benson said with a slight blush. "Jeff was telling me some of his parlor jokes. Pool parlor, if you ask me."

Jeff Ring pooh-poohed. Sally Peterson made a face. "If you laugh at Jeff's so-called jokes, Eva, you ought to see a head-shrinker."

"Where were you when it happened, Mr. Turnboldt?" Corrigan asked politely.

"In my office, trying to think up a toothpaste slogan." The copywriter indicated the door into the north room of the suite. "Jeff and I share the hole."

"You were in there alone?"

Turnboldt shrugged. "You heard Jeff. He was out here with Eva."

Corrigan picked up the lantern again and went to the indicated door. The office used by Turnboldt and Ring was too large for only two men, and an abysmal clutter. Desks stood front to front; each was flanked by a typewriter stand.

The room was not rectangular. A sizable right angle bitten out of the wall at the far end, on the corridor side, evidently was occupied by the ladies' room, entrance to which was from the public hall. Along the same wall another chunk projected; this one had a door from the copywriters' office, and Corrigan went over and looked in. It was a stockroom, evidently for the entire agency.

The office was in the northwest corner of the twenty-first floor. Brian Frank's office occupied the northeast section, with the public hall between; their rear windows faced the north side of the building. For someone with no fear of heights it would have been a simple matter to let himself out of Turnboldt's and Ring's rear window onto the ledge and inch along the ledge to the murdered accountant's window and into his office. The distance was not great; there was small chance that anyone would spot the killer from the street, and the next building to the north was ten floors shorter; the only danger the ledge-walker ran was in possibly being spotted as he passed the window of the public hall going and coming back, and a little caution and luck would obviate that.

Corrigan went back into the reception room.

They were all waiting in a kind of bewilderment, as if they could not imagine why he should be going to all this trouble over a suicide. "Did you hear the shot, Mr. Turnboldt?"

"Nope," Turnboldt said promptly.

"Was your rear window open?" Corrigan had noticed on his survey that the rear window was closed.

"Not in this weather. The only thing I heard was Eva laughing at Jeff's bum joke. She stopped in the middle of a laugh and I heard Sybil's voice, all excited. That brought me out into the reception room. The three of them were dashing into the hall. I ran after them to see what was the matter."

"Well, that's clear enough." Corrigan's face showed nothing, and his one eye was as unblinking as a locomotive headlight. It turned on the blonde. "And where were you, Miss Peterson?"

"In my studio," the artist said. Then she shrugged. "Quite alone, I might add. So I can't prove it, though why anyone should have to prove anything is beyond me, Captain. Maybe you know what you're doing, but I don't."

"I'd like to see your studio."

She shrugged again, rose, and went to the entrance of the office hall that bisected the south wall of the agency reception room. Corrigan pushed through the gate in the railing and followed with the lantern.

For once Chuck Baer did not accompany him. Corrigan noticed him eying the liquor on the makeshift bar. He envied the big lug. Chuck was setting himself for a slug. No reason why he shouldn't; there were no rules against drinking in his line of work. Lucky stiff, he thought.

The hallway along which the woman artist led Corrigan ran parallel to the public corridor, with offices to each side. They passed two doors almost immediately: the one to the left was unmarked (probably another office for copywriters! Corrigan thought—a guess immediately substantiated by the Peterson woman); the one to the right was inscribed CHARLES HARDER, ACCOUNT EXECUTIVE. There was a far more impressive door farther down the hall, on the same side as the account executive's, lettered MILTON J.J. ADAMS, PRESIDENT. Directly across the hall from Adam's office was a door lettered ART DEPARTMENT. It was at this door that Sally Peterson stopped.

She opened it and stepped in before him, Corrigan holding the Coleman high. It was a spacious studio with two very large windows facing the south, the street side of the building. She noticed Corrigan glancing that way and laughed. "I tried to tell J.J. that an artist needs north light, not south, but he got this suite cheap on a long-term lease, and he said I'd have to make do. You'll just love Milton J.J. Adams, Captain, if you stick around that long."

Corrigan said nothing. He went to one of the windows—both were shut—opened it, and looked down. There was the ledge.

He closed the window and looked around.

Artwork was stacked everywhere—on easels, on the floor, against the wall. He noticed a door in the wall opposite the windows and went over to see what lay beyond. It was the second copywriters' office. Its east wall ran along the public corridor, its west wall along the agency hallway, while its north wall separated it from the reception room and its south wall from Sally Peterson's office—there were no windows.

Sally Peterson laughed her brittle laugh again. "We call it the Black Hole around here," she said. "The poor guys have to work by artificial light all day. J.J., of course, says artificial light is better than sunlight. Oh, you'll adore him."

Corrigan went back into the studio and over to a door that, from its position, led to the public corridor; this must be the door he had noted immediately to his left when he and Chuck Baer had stepped out of the emergency stairway into the twenty-first floor. He opened it and looked out; yes, that was the one, unmarked from the corridor side. Directly opposite was the door to Laverne Thomas's office; diagonally across the hall was the entrance to 2102, Griswald Jewelers. He shut the door; it locked automatically.

Sally seated herself on a studio couch; a moment later she stretched out on it. Her skirt hiked up her thighs. She had sexy legs; she's got into the habit of showing them off, he thought, and grinned to himself. She was watching him, possibly for a reaction. Keep watching, baby!

If she was the one who had rigged the fake

suicide, she had had a long, long tippy-toe along that ledge. If, that is, she had started her journey from one of her two windows. It would have meant going halfway around the building if she had gone east and north, and about three-quarters of the way around the building if she had gone west, north, and east. Even assuming the shorter route, it would have meant passing Laverne Thomas's south window and east window, the two windows of the Griswald Jewelers' display room, the window of Everett Griswald's office, and the windows of Carleton Burns's office before she reached the east window into the accountants' office of Burns Accounting. The risks of being spotted were enormous. And, aside from that, he could not see a woman negotiating a narrow ledge for such a considerable distance at an altitude of twenty-one floors above the street.

Of course, Sally Peterson could have left her studio by the door into the public hall, walked the length of the hall to the north end, and climbed out the hall window; then she would have had only a few feet to negotiate to the north window of Brian Frank's office. That made more sense. But not much conviction.

He let it lie. This was a number-one toughie to figure.

"When did you learn about the shooting, Miss Peterson?"

"I was getting ready to leave, Captain, heading toward the ladies' room to freshen up, when I passed the open door to Burns Accounting and saw Jeff and Eva, Tony, and Sybil Graves all crowded around the door to Brian's office. I never did get to powder my nose. Naturally I joined the others to see what was wrong.''

"Well," he said pleasantly. "That clears that much up. Let's get back to the others."

But she did not move from the couch.

"Captain," she said. She was sitting up now, and the movement had drawn her skirt down. He did not think, from the hesitation in her voice and the seriousness of her expression, that she was thinking about her sex appeal now.

"Yes?" Corrigan said. He wondered what was coming.

"I called you Captain Kidd before. That was a nasty thing to say. I despise people who call attention to other people's infirmities.''

"That's all right, Miss Peterson. We get used to it."

"No, please. For some reason—maybe it's this damn blackout—I want you to understand that I'm not really the way I sometimes sound. I learned long ago in this town that you have to keep up a front if you want to stay in the rat race. The front I chose was the woman-of-the-world pose—you know, a crack for every situation.''

"I've met plenty of those," he said with a smile.

"The truth is, Captain, I'm a complete fraud. I walk around scared half to death most of the time. The more scared I get, the more my tongue betrays me. This blackout . . ." She looked around at the shadows the lantern was casting, at the almost unrelieved blackness of the city beyond her windows, and shivered. "It has me terrified. Do you suppose they're putting out deliberately false reports on the radio?"

"Why would they do that, Miss Peterson?"

"Maybe they're trying to prevent panic by hiding the truth."

"About what?"

"About—" he could hardly hear her voice—"the world's coming to an end or something."

"I doubt if the conspiracy could be that widespread, Miss Peterson," he said with another smile.

"Or do you suppose it could be—World War III?"

"If anyone'd dropped a hydrogen bomb," Corrigan said dryly, "we'd hardly be holding this conversation."

"I know; you think I'm a stupid broad. I don't blame you. But it could be sabotage."

"That," he said, "is always a possibility. Look, Miss Peterson, we're grownup people, and we live on a tightrope, and if anyone's found a way to get us back to solid ground again I haven't heard of it. We're all in the same bind, the whole damn planet, and maybe that's what's going to save us. Anyway, there's nothing you or I can do about it. Shall we go?"

She swung her legs to the floor, gripping the couch, staring at him. Suddenly she jumped up, laughing, and said, "Why not? This could be a gas. But don't be surprised if in three minutes I'm my old bitchy self again, Captain."

"I won't," Corrigan said, and he let her precede him to the door.

It could be a gas, he thought. It could also be a clever female move to get under his crust to the soft parts. He shrugged and closed the door from the hall side.

9.

Corrigan asked Wanda Hitchey where she had been at the time of the shooting. The file clerk of the ad agency gave him her sultriest look.

"In the powder room up the hall," she said. "Just as I came out I saw Sally go into Burns Accounting. I wondered why, and I glanced in. When I saw everybody in there, I went in, too."

"Did you hear the shot, Miss Hitchey? You may have been in the ladies' room when it went off."

"I may have," the girl said. "I have the feeling I recall a kind of sharp popping sound, but I didn't think anything of it at the time. I didn't think anything about it at all. Like you wouldn't pay attention to a door slamming somewhere."

Corrigan sighed. "How long were you in the ladies' room, would you say?"

"Oh, I don't know, Captain. A few minutes, maybe."

Plump Mrs. Eva Benson said, "You left here at twenty-five to five, Wanda. You always do. You know you do."

The overmade-up girl glared at her.

"Well, you do," little Dutchie said stubbornly. "You head for that powder room the minute Mr. Adams leaves for the day. I don't care if you goof off the last forty minutes every day; I'm not paying your salary. But don't say just a few minutes. I don't know what you do in that powder room— goodness, I could take a bath, change my clothes, make up, and take a nap in the time you spend in there."

The office siren tossed her auburn locks. "You could afford to spend some time on yourself, dearie. How you ever snagged a man I'll never understand. You always look like something the cat dragged in."

"Maybe it's because I don't try as hard as some people I could mention," the little receptionist retorted. She pointed to one of the desks on the other side of the railing. "That's her desk, Captain. I can't help noticing when she leaves the room. We're supposed to work until a quarter past five. She always heads for that powder room about twenty-five to. *Always*."

Corrigan held up a restraining hand. God bless the blackout.

"Did you hear anyone outside in the hall while you were in the ladies' room, Miss Hitchey?"

She continued to glare at Eva Benson. "No," she snapped. "Water was running and things."

"Did anyone else enter while you were in there?"

She shook her head.

So Wanda Hitchey could have used the window

at the end of the public hall to reach Brian Frank's office; it was just outside the door of the ladies' room. From the standpoint of opportunity, he now had three suspects from the Adams Advertising Agency: Tony Turnboldt, Sally Peterson, and Wanda Hitchey. Always bearing in mind that he had an even better suspect in Sybil Graves, with no fancy business about windows and ledges.

It was possible, of course, that someone who had left one of the offices earlier had sneaked back to commit the murder, escaping observation. Or that some complete outsider had stepped off the elevator, used the window at the rear of the hall to get to Brian Frank's office, then made it back to the elevator or the stairs at the opposite end of the hall before Sybil rushed across to the agency office for help.

After swift reflection, Corrigan dismissed this last possibility on two grounds. First, the killer had to know where old Griswald kept his pistol, which was unlikely for an outsider. More important, the killer not only had to be familiar with the layout of the offices and the availability of the ledge; he would also have had to know that Brian Frank was working overtime today. Since presumably Frank himself hadn't known this until the moment he decided to finish the report he was working on, this pretty well restricted the suspects to those still on the floor; and to those who had left early—the accountant who worked with Frank, the man named Gil Stoner; Carleton Burns, the head of the accountancy firm; and old Everett Griswald himself, whose P38 had been used in the killing.

Corrigan felt that he now had all the information he was likely to get from the people trapped with him on the twenty-first floor. The obvious next move was to dig into possible motives. What, if any, had been the dead man's relationship with the various suspects? It was the kind of information far likelier to be given in confidence than in a group.

"I guess that pretty well winds things up," he said. "As far as I'm concerned, you can all go back to your party."

Predictably, it was Tony Turnboldt who jumped up first. "Time for another drinkee, guys and dolls. Bring your cups to the bar!"

He promptly followed his own advice. He fished a couple of melting ice cubes from the cellophane bag and mixed himself a Scotch and soda. The others came over for refills. Chatter filled the office.

Baer gave him an imperceptible nod as he strolled over to the bar; he knew what Corrigan had in mind. Ignored for the moment, Corrigan had a quiet word with the two police officers. They watched him approach them with apprehension. Corrigan's reputation as a stickler for competent work was known throughout the department.

Corrigan gave Maloney and Coats his frostiest look.

"Something wrong, Captain?" the older patrolman asked uneasily.

"As if you didn't know, Maloney. I could maybe find excuses for young Coats here, but not a cop with your experience. How do you explain a working team that didn't even know a pair of witnesses had left the scene of a crime till they'd been gone three-quarters of an hour?"

"You mean Mr. Turnboldt and Mr. Ring, when they went out for the chow?" Maloney asked, shifting his feet.

"Yes, that's just what I mean."

"Captain." Maloney wet his lips. "We instructed them to stay put. We had to stay with the body—"

"You could have split up."

"Yeah. I'm sorry, Captain. Anyway, they did come back."

"I'm not objecting to their going out after some food," Corrigan growled. "There would have been nothing wrong with your giving them permission to do that. What I'm stepping on you for is that you didn't know they were gone."

"Yes, sir," both men muttered.

Corrigan looked them over for a moment. Suddenly the chill went out of his eye. "Okay, that's that. Did you both get enough to eat?"

Young Coats's jaw dropped. Maloney let out his breath; it was over. He knew enough about Corrigan's reputation to recognize the signs. Corrigan stepped hard on goofers but, having stepped, he dismissed the matter from his mind.

Maloney said they had had plenty of food, and Coats bobbed his head hastily.

"What do you want us to do now, Captain?" Maloney asked.

"Stand by, I may need you."

"Yes, sir. I thought you'd ended the investigation for tonight."

"Hardly," Corrigan said dryly. "For one thing, we can't just walk off and leave that body. You'll have to stick around till the power comes back on and somebody comes after it."

Officer Coats said timidly, "We go off duty at midnight, Captain."

"Not if the power is still off. I doubt that headquarters can send replacements. About eleven-thirty you can phone in and try your luck, but my guess is you're both stuck. If you want, you can try to catch some sleep over at Burns Accounting. How long will that lantern burn?"

"Five, six hours, sir. It was full. We lit it about twenty to six, when we started up the stairs."

Corrigan looked at his watch. It was ten past eight, which meant the lantern had been burning for two and a half hours.

"Maybe we'd better conserve fuel," he said. "No telling when we may need it."

He screwed the fuel valve closed. As the lantern dimmed to a flicker and died, leaving the three candles lighting the office, everyone looked startled—everyone but Tony Turnboldt.

"Great idea, Captain," Turnboldt laughed. "Candlelight's a lot more romantic."

He slipped his arm about Sally Peterson's waist. She side-stepped neatly and moved over to Chuck Baer, who looked pleased. Turnboldt laughed again and grabbed Wanda Hitchey by the hand.

"Let's try again for a dance band, baby." He led her over to the desk where he had parked the transistor radio.

Corrigan ambled over to the group at the bar. Pudgy Jeff Ring offered him a drink. He shook his head. "Ginger ale," he said. Sybil Graves, sipping a bourbon and soda, walked around to him as he sampled it.

"Aren't you off duty now, Captain? Can't you have a drink?"

Dance music suddenly burst from the radio. Turnboldt pushed desks away to clear a space in the middle of the outer office, and turned to Wanda. She was already gyrating her shoulders and doing little bumps in the oddly aseptic isolation of the modern dance. The office Lothario would have none of it.

"I feel like contact, baby," he said, and pulled her to him. The girl smiled lazily up at him. They began moving slowly, as close-fitting as a tree graft.

Corrigan tried not to watch them. This was duty, and no time to give in to the eternal itch. Still, it was to his official advantage to keep them all thinking that he was only hanging around because of the blackout and the "suicide's" body. So why not?

"I'd rather dance than drink," Corrigan said to the Irish girl. "How about it?"

She looked at him, the usual feminine speculative look. He felt a rising excitement.

"Why not?" Sybil Graves said, raising her arms to him. "It's not every day a girl gets to dance with a real live detective."

Her tilted little nose came about even with his

chin. He was conscious of her breasts against his body. He was also conscious of Chuck Baer's amused glance.

"You're as light as a summer breeze," he said into her ear.

"Thank you, sir," Sybil murmured. "You're no clod yourself."

"If you don't quit calling me sir, I'll pop you out on that ledge."

"Ledge?"

"Never mind. I'm not all that older than you." She drew back to hold him at arms' length, looking solemnly up at him. He was glad she was not being coy. "I don't remember your first name, if I ever heard it."

"Tim," he said.

"Tim," she nodded. "That's just right for you. I like it."

"Since I'm sort of off duty, I don't mind admitting I like Sybil."

"If I'm not to call you Captain Corrigan any more, you're not to call me Miss Graves any more."

"Okay, Sybil it is."

He drew her close, and she buried her face in his shoulder. They danced dreamily.

Some case, he thought. By candlelight, yet!

10.

The piece ended; there was a commercial. As Corrigan and the girl walked back to where they had left their drinks, he was astonished to see Chuck Baer and Sally Peterson still dancing to the sound of music apparently only they could hear. The blonde had her eyes shut, and Baer had a silly look on his face. My God, it's got to Chuck, too! Corrigan thought. Only a major catastrophe could have made him dance in public. He was about as graceful as a performing bear.

Sybil's cup was nearly empty.

"Refill?" Corrigan asked her.

She gave a little giggle. "I'm not sure I ought to."

"Why not?"

"Anything over ten sips is out of bounds for me."

"What happens to you?"

"I'm not going to tell you. You're not drinking at all. That's ginger ale straight, isn't it?"

"Yes. But I'm worse than you. I can't take even one." Corrigan could drink any man in the department under the table. The only one who could keep up with him was Baer, whose capacity was like Thor's.

"Then don't you dare," the little Irish girl said. "But me . . . I don't know, Tim, I feel sort of reckless tonight. I wonder why." He knew why; it was the blackout. "I think I'll have just one more."

"All right." By the time he brought her a refill, the music had started again. Baer and the Peterson woman were still swaying in the middle of the floor. Eva Benson, the ad agency receptionist, was being pulled onto the floor by Jeff Ring, Turnboldt's co-copywriter. Ring's attitude seemed to be: Any port in a storm. From the look he sent their way, it was obvious that he would have preferred Sybil.

Wanda Hitchey and Tony Turnboldt, from their movements, were working up to something. And all of a sudden Corrigan saw Chuck Baer leave the floor with Sally Peterson and steer her through the gate in the railing across the reception room and into the agency hall. I wonder whose idea that was? Corrigan thought. Considering the pair involved, it was a tossup. That they were headed for Sally's studio—in the dark—he never doubted.

Neat little Howard Craft in his bifocals and knife-edge trousers was seated primly on the reception-area sofa, cup in hand, staring straight ahead. Beside him sat his co-worker of Griswald Jewelers, gray-haired Laverne Thomas. Her cup of whatever it was looked untouched. They simply sat there side by side, without conversation; they might have been in separate rooms. Instinct told Corrigan that something was bothering both of them. What was it? He noticed Craft take a sudden swig and inch a little closer to the Thomas woman. She seemed astounded. But she did not move away.

Sybil asked Corrigan for a cigaret; he gave her one and held a light for her. He went for an ashtray, and she followed him and perched on the railing.

"Your friend Mr. Baer's a fast worker," Sybil remarked.

Corrigan glanced toward the dark hallway. Sally Peterson and the big redhead had disappeared.

"Maybe it's your friend Sally who's the fast worker."

She shrugged. "Sally's not my friend." She added quickly, "I mean, we get along and all that, but I just don't know her well. Our only contact is here at the office."

"What's the hangup between Sally and Wanda Hitchey?" he asked carelessly.

Sybil glanced over at the sexy file clerk in the arms of Turnboldt. "You noticed?"

"I've got forty-forty vision in my one eye."

Sybil took a sip of her drink. "They're sort of ex-rivals."

"Ex?"

"For poor Brian. The man who shot himself."

Corrigan felt himself turn all cop again.

Statistically, the triangle was among the common-est of murder motives. He wondered what little Irish would think of him if she had known he was deliberately working on her.

"You class them as ex-rivals just because the guy's dead?"

"Oh, no. The competition flopped while he was still alive. Sally gave Brian the heave when she found out he was making out with Wanda on the sly. Then Wanda threw Brian over, with fire-works, when she learned that he was cheating on her with a married woman.

"Sounds as though the late Mr. Frank was quite a hand with the ladies."

"Was he ever! He hardly ever gave up when he was hunting for somebody to jump into bed with. And he was always out on that little old trail with gun and camera. It's true Brian was kind of good-looking and had a certain sneaky charm, but when a man makes a pass at practically every girl he meets, by the law of averages he's bound to get a good percentage of takers. He was pretty success-ful."

Corrigan looked down at her. "Every girl?"

Her creamy Irish skin grew strawberries. "Sure, he went after me, too. After all, I was the handiest—I worked in the same office. But I wasn't one of the takers, Captain Corrigan, if that's what you had in mind."

Of course not, he thought immediately; not this girl. And an instant later he was dressing himself down for falling for a preconception. Sybil Graves was still his main suspect. If she was the one who

101

had plugged Frank, she had had a reason; and the standard reason was under his nose. Naturally she would lie.

And all the time he was going through these mental gymnastics something was insisting—a small, annoying, not-to-be-stilled voice—that the whole notion was nonsense.

He found himself going over a list of top-flight criminal lawyers he knew.

Damn! How had he got himself emotionally involved with this hundred pounds of Irish dynamite?

"I'd like to hear the peeping details, Sybil. I mean of Frank's romantic progress from Sally to Wanda to this married woman."

She looked at him. "I wouldn't have suspected you of being interested in gossip."

"It's part of being a cop. You forget I'm investigating a man's death."

"I thought you'd finished doing that."

He smiled at her. "I just reached a point where nothing more could be done till the lab technicians could look things over. Sort of marking time."

"Oh." She snubbed her cigaret out in the tray between them. "You're looking for some motive for Brian's suicide."

"Something like that." It was even tough to lie to her!

"Wait—a—minute." She was staring at him out of widening blue eyes. "I've been wondering why you've avoided using the word suicide. You don't think it's a suicide at all, do you? Do you?"

"I didn't say—"

"I know what you *didn't* say. And all this time you've been pumping me!" The blue eyes were filling with horror. "You even think—you think that I—"

He had to look away, cursing himself. "I don't think anything," he said lamely. "My job is to get at facts. I'm not in the enviable position of the Tony Turnboldts of this town."

"But no one else was there! If Brian didn't shoot himself, you're accusing *me!*"

He was thinking desperately of some ways to restore his psychological advantage. If Inspector Macelyn down at MOS ever got wind of the way he was handling this!

"Look, Sybil," he heard himself saying. "There's a two-foot ledge that runs around the twenty-first floor under the windows. Both windows in Frank's office were unlatched. It's theoretically possible for someone to walk along the ledge to his office, then leave by the same route."

He was relieved to note that the notion threw her. Or—always the reservation!—seemed to.

"But then—that would mean he was—you mean he was *murdered?*" Corrigan was very glad she whispered it.

"Now, did I say that, Sybil? It's just that I have to keep an open mind. That's why I've got to learn everything I can about Frank's relationships with the rest of the people on the floor."

She drained her cup abruptly and handed it to Corrigan. "You've got me all upset. I want another drink."

"Sure," he said.

The disc on the radio ended as Corrigan was mixing her drink. When he got back to Sybil, Ring was asking her for the next dance.

"Not right now, Jeff," Sybil was saying. "I'm talking to Tim."

"Tim?" The copywriter glanced owlishly at Corrigan. "Oh, the cop. Sorry, Off'sher. Di'n't know I was interrupting shome—something."

Ring lurched back to the bar and yanked Wanda Hitchey to his prominent belly. "C'mere, you luscious thing, you. Boy, do I go for you. I bet you and me could make shweet mushic—music—"

"Right now, Jeffie, you couldn't make a department store dummy. Better go easy on that Russian lightning." The file clerk patted his cheek and turned to Turnboldt, who was grinning then.

"What's with Ring?" Corrigan asked Sybil. "Aside from being loaded, I mean. He have a thing for you?"

"He's never shown it before," the girl said, looking puzzled. "I'm not exactly flattered. The guy has a wife and four kids."

"It's the office-party atmosphere."

"More likely the blackout," Sybil said. "You know, Tim, it's funny. I've never felt like this in my life. Sort of—oh, like a carnival, where anything goes, and to heck with tomorrow. I'm usually a pretty levelheaded gal, and here I am way over my quota!" She looked at the cup he had handed her. "And I don't seem to care. Don't you feel it?"

Irish, if you only knew! Corrigan thought

104

fervently. "It's my training, I guess," he said, wishing it were. "Practical guy, you know. I keep thinking the lights will come back on any minute. But I'm a native New Yorker. Your accent tells me you're from the Middle West."

"Ames, Iowa," she nodded. "But what has that to do with anything?"

"New Yorkers are like Pavlov's dogs—we have a conditioned reflex where public utilities are concerned. A failure of electric power in a city like this is unthinkable. But you come from tornado country, where the lights, and everything else, can go out any time."

"That ought to make us panicky."

"Where do you think your carnival-the-hell-with-tomorrow feeling comes from?" he asked her dryly.

"Oh," she said, and fell silent.

At that moment Turnboldt, in the act of mixing himself another drink, glanced around and inquired loudly, "What happened to our gal Sal?"

The music had come on again; Ring had managed to embrace Wanda and was clowning about the floor with her; she was laughing her head off and rubbing up to him maliciously. Eva Benson was back behind her desk, looking faintly appalled. Then she took a quick drink.

It was Laverne Thomas, still seated beside Howard Craft on the sofa, who said, "Miss Peterson and that Mr. Baer went down the hall."

Corrigan frowned after him. "Is Sally Peterson Turnboldt's girl friend?"

"He's married, too," Sybil said.

105

"That's hardly what I asked you."

Sybil hesitated. "I *hate* talking about people. . . . I've heard gossip that there was something between them about a year ago, when Sally first joined the Adams agency. The story was that Tony was separated from his wife at the time, then decided to go back to her. I really don't know much about it, Tim. I wasn't working for Burns Accounting then."

From where they sat on the railing they could see down the hall. In the glow of the candle, Corrigan saw Turnboldt open the studio door and go in without knocking. The hall became a tunnel again as the door closed behind him.

Corrigan grinned. If Terrible Tony intended to create a scene, it was too bad Chuck's fun would be interrupted, but it was Turnboldt who would pay. Nothing less than a collapsing building was likely to bruise Mr. Baer, and the extent of Turnboldt's injuries would depend entirely on how obnoxious he made himself. He listened for sounds of carnage and heard none.

"Let's get back to what we were talking about," he said to Sybil.

"All right," she said. "What were we talking about?"

"The love life of Brian Frank."

11.

Sybil took a sip of her drink. "Brian was romancing Sally when I came to work for Burns Accounting a few months ago. He'd just started going with her. Before that he'd been rushing the girl who'd had my job. The floor scuttle is that she quit with a broken heart because Brian dropped her."

"Did you ever meet this girl?"

"For a couple of days. She broke me in."

"Any idea where she is now?"

"Not the slightest. You know," Sybil said thoughtfully, "I felt awfully sorry for her. Brian was the kind of s.o.b. who'd pick the easy ones between heavy affairs. This poor girl had had polio as a child and she had to wear a brace. He apparently got a kick out of it."

Aside from what this told him about Frank's character, such as it was, Sybil's information eliminated her predecessor as a possible murderess. No one dragging a leg in a brace could have negotiated that ledge.

Corrigan said, "If Sally Peterson's worked here for a year, how come it took Brian Frank so long to get around to her? Was it because of her thing with Tony Turnboldt?"

Her blue eyes danced. "A good detective ought to be able to figure that out."

"Got it," he said. "Frank hadn't worked here very long—anywhere near as long as Sally."

The girl raised her cup in a silent toast to his acumen.

There was the slightest slur in her voice; the liquor she had consumed was beginning to affect her. He wished she would stop drinking; he hated women who got drunk.

"How long had Frank been with Burns Accounting?"

"Oh, about four months."

"You mean that in just four months he had romances with the girl you replaced, with Sally Peterson, with Wanda Hitchey, and with that married woman you mentioned? Quite a stud. Has he missed anything in skirts on the twenty-first floor?"

Her glance went to Laverne Thomas, seated on the sofa beside Howard Craft. "Not many."

"Who was the married woman?"

"You're pumping me, Captain," Sybil said just the least bit uncertainly.

"Just talking," Corrigan said. "I've found myself getting interested in these people. You don't have to tell me, Sybil. I'll find out easily enough."

She shrugged, and her mammae followed suit. He forced himself to look away. "Well, it's no top secret. Gil Stoner's wife."

He was surprised. "The wife of the accountant who worked in the same office with Frank?"

"That's the one."

"What a man," Corrigan said casually. "I suppose Stoner didn't know it? The husband's usually the last to find out."

"He found out yesterday. Or I suppose it must have been over the weekend that he found out. But the blowoff came yesterday morning."

"Sounds interesting. Maybe you'd better give me a chronological rundown on this guy Frank's amorous adventures. Start with Sally."

"I don't know why I'm letting you turn me into a—a canary," Sybil murmured, "but for some reason I don't seem to care. From what I've gathered, Sally had no idea Brian was the Don Juan he was. She knew about Helen something-or-other, my predecessor—I've forgotten her last name—but two affairs don't necessarily make a man a wolf. Sally, and everybody else on the floor except me, seemed under the impression that she and Brian were eventually going to be married."

"Everybody except you?"

"He was still on the sly asking me out. So I knew he was a born cheat." Sybil raised her cup, and then set it definitely down. Apparently she had decided that discretion was the better part of toping. Corrigan felt a great relief. "It's funny, but I think he was really fond of Sally; maybe he did intend to marry her. He seemed quite upset when Sally found out he was secretly dating Wanda and threw him over."

"But not upset enough to give up Wanda," Corrigan said dryly.

"I think he would have. I do know he tried to make up with Sally. But I guess Sally realized then that he was an incurable chaser and would have nothing further to do with him. It was only when Brian saw there was no hope of getting Sally back that he began dating Wanda openly."

"How long ago was that?"

"A couple of weeks ago."

"And then Wanda in turn bounced him because he cheated on her with Stoner's wife?"

"Yes, but I'm sure Wanda would have taken him back. She made such a scene Brian wouldn't even speak to her. But that was only yesterday. In time they'd both have simmered down. Anyway, that's my opinion."

"Exactly what happened yesterday?"

"Well, the first scene was at eight-thirty, just after I'd opened the office. Gil was the first one in after me. He barely spoke to me. I assumed it was Monday morning blues and thought nothing of it. He went into his and Brian's office and shut the door. Two minutes later Brian showed up, and the fireworks started the minute he got into their office. I heard Gil yell, 'You lousy homewrecker! I ought to knock your—' I'm not going to repeat his language, but you can imagine."

Corrigan smiled. "You'll have to if it comes to a

written statement, but skip it for now. Then what happened?"

"I didn't hear Brian's reply, but apparently he made one, because there was a rather long pause before Gil started shouting at him again. I couldn't help hearing everything he said. It seemed Mrs. Stoner had confessed to having gone to bed with Brian. Gil ended by yelling, 'I'll fix your wagon!' along with a string of dirty words; then he stormed out and went across the hall."

"To the ad agency?"

"I wondered why, too. I understood when Gil came marching back with Wanda a few minutes later."

"He'd run over to snitch on Frank?"

"You *are* a detective, Captain Corrigan."

Interestingly untypical. The typical male reaction would have been to take some violent physical action against the man who had cuckolded him. But Gil Stoner hadn't even thrown a punch at the befouler of his nest. Instead, like a vindictive small boy, he had run across the hall to tell tales to another of the man's mistresses.

It was so untypical that Corrigan wondered. Could it have been a cover-up, a premeditated action to make himself look unmanly, while all the time he was planning Frank's murder? Or Stoner could have taken a characteristic course in blabbing to the Hitchey girl, then worked himself up into a lather as he brooded over the affair. In either case he could have sneaked back after openly leaving at 4:30. Or maybe he never left the building

111

at all. He might simply have got off the elevator on the twentieth floor, climbed the stairs back to the twenty-first, and hidden somewhere until he felt he had a clear field.

"Then what happened?" Corrigan asked Sybil.

"Gil tore open the door into his and Brian's office and stepped aside for Wanda. She stood there in the doorway and told Brian off in very unladylike language. She called him every four-letter word I ever heard, and a lot that were brand-new to me. What it all added up to was that she never wanted to see him again. Then she did an about-face and marched across the hall to the ladies' room, I suppose to have herself a good cry. Mr. Burns hadn't come in yet, or Brian would have been fired. Mr. Burns is a pretty conservative old man, and such goings-on would have appalled him."

"He still doesn't know of the disturbance?"

Sybil shook her head. "By the time he got in, Brian was down the hall at Griswald Jewelers checking their inventory statement against the stock; that's part of a really good audit, you know. Gil was working alone in the office they shared. Needless to say, nobody mentioned the ruckus to Mr. Burns."

"When Frank got back from Griswald's, these two guys continued to work in the same room?" Corrigan said unbelievingly.

"I suppose they really had no choice in the matter, unless one was willing to quit his job. I guess neither was."

Corrigan was silent. Then he said, "I assume you have Gil Stoner's home phone number in your office?" She nodded, and he got to his feet. "Let's go over."

Sybil took one look into the blackness of the public hall and balked. "Aren't you going to bring the lantern, or at least a candle?"

He grinned and produced his pencil flashlight, took her hand, and led her like a child. Her hand, as small as a child's, snuggled confidently in his paw. It feels too damned good, Corrigan told himself masochistically, and he was actually relieved when he had to let go of it to open the door to the Burns Accounting Company.

"There's a phone list pasted to my desk top," Sybil said innocently. But then she glanced at the closed door to the accountants' room and gave a little shiver. She was subdued after that.

There were several dozen names on the list. Opposite *Stoner, Gilbert* was typed a number with a Brooklyn exchange.

"Where in Brooklyn does Stoner live, do you know?"

"The Prospect Park section."

"Does he drive in?"

"No. He's always complaining about the conditions in the subway."

A twenty- to twenty-five-minute ride—twenty-five at tops. Corrigan pondered. It shouldn't have taken Stoner more than fifteen minutes from the time he left the office until he was on a train. Probably not more than half that. But stretch it

113

and grant him fifteen. At the latest he should have been getting off at his Brooklyn station by ten after five. Any way you looked at it, it would have been a good ten minutes or more before the power went out. So if he was home now, it would be pretty good evidence that he couldn't have been still hanging around the Bower Building at three minutes past five, when Frank was shot. *If* Stoner was home now.

Directing his light at the phone, Corrigan got the number. The buzzes at the other end stopped in the

"Hello?" a woman's voice said in a petulant tone.

"Mr. Stoner, please," Corrigan asked.

"He never got home tonight. He's probably caught in one of the stalled subway trains."

"Oh. I thought he'd have made it to Brooklyn before the power failure. Doesn't he usually get home by a few minutes past five?"

"A few minutes past six, you mean!"

Corrigan made himself sound doubtful. "Oh," he said. "I thought he got off work at four-thirty."

"He does," the woman told him. "But you don't know that husband of mine if you think he ever comes straight home. He has to stop for his beers first. Who is this?"

Corrigan saw no point in telling her he was a police officer. "My name's Corrigan. We've never met, Mrs. Stoner."

"Corrigan? Never heard. What do you want Gil for?"

"It's nothing that won't keep until tomorrow.

Thanks, Mrs. Stoner." He hung up before she could ask another question.

That leaves Stoner in the running, Corrigan thought. Unless he can establish that he'd been in some pub at 5:03 P.M.

He said to Sybil, "Let's get back to the party."

12.

Chuck Baer had early become conscious of the blonde Peterson woman's interest in him. It was nothing more than a certain speculation in her eye on the two occasions when he caught her giving him the once-over, but that was enough. Baer had never felt false modesty about his attractiveness to women; he accepted it as a fringe benefit of his ugliness, and he had few scruples about taking advantage of it. The man-woman freak-out was like any war; you had an objective, and if you were a good man you let nothing stand in your way.

So he showed no surprise, and felt none, when Sally Peterson shook off Tony Turnboldt's arm and walked over to him.

"You don't have a cup, Mr. Baer. Don't you drink?"

"Nobody's offered me one," Baer said, smiling. "And I'm not exactly an invited guest."

"What do you drink?" Turnboldt asked in a chilly voice.

The redhead told him bourbon and soda, agreeably. The handsome copywriter obliged, and mixed one for Sally, too. He seemed disposed to hang around; but she turned her back on him, and he stalked away.

"Tell me about yourself, Mr. Baer," Sally said. "I've never met a real live private eye before."

"Whatever I told you would be a lie," Baer said. "It's one of the dullest jobs there is. But if you insist—like what?"

"Well, for a starter, like whether you're single or married."

"I wouldn't lie to you about that," he grinned. "I'm not even engaged." He glanced at her left hand.

"Detecting, too, Mr. Baer?" Sally murmured. "I'm also unattached, for what it's worth."

"What is it worth?"

"Now you wouldn't want me to tell you that. Really, Mr. Baer! That would take all the Moxie out of it."

So Moxie's coming back, he thought. After all, she was in the ad race. Things began to look up. He had never made a play for a commercial artist before.

They fenced about for a few minutes. When Turnboldt located some more dance music and sailed off with Wanda Hitchey, Sally Peterson murmured, "Do I have to call you Mr. Baer?"

"Mr. Baer was my father," Baer said solemnly. "My handle is Chuck. I was about to insist on it."

She put out her hand. "Mine's Sally." He shook it, and held on.

117

She did not seem to mind. She glanced over to the dancers. "Shall we join them?"

"I have two left feet. But if your toes can stand it, I'll give it a whirl."

Sally promptly took the cup from his hand and carried it and her own to the nearest desk. Then she came back and held out her arms, smiling. He braced himself, shook his head like a bear, and drew her to him.

He was astounded to find himself moving about the floor like a pro. What a dancer she was!

"Hey," he said. "You're making even me enjoy this."

"I love to dance."

"I'm beginning to realize the advantages." He squeezed her to him, but she shook her head, laughing, and drew away.

"Wrestling is for Madison Square Garden, Chuck. If you want to dance, let's dance. If you want to wrestle . . ."

They moved back to the desk to reclaim their drinks.

"How come you're unattached, Sally?"

She said lightly, "It's a sad tale. Let's talk about something else."

"Aren't you dating at all?"

"I haven't been out with a man in over two weeks."

"It must be by choice. Or the men in your life aren't men. How come?"

"Oh, the last one happens to be married. I'm hoping that news of my unattached state eventually reaches my single men friends. My status is fairly recent. Up till a couple of weeks ago I was more or less engaged."

He cocked a red brow at her. "How do you become more or less engaged? It's like being more or less pregnant."

"Oh, you have a sort of unspelled-out understanding. The man never says anything really binding, but you both get into the habit of remarking how many children you'd like, how big an apartment you'd need, that sort of thing. Anyway, that's what fooled me."

"The guy is a heel. Now me, I make a point of letting my women know off the bat that I'm a confirmed bachelor."

She laughed. "Okay, Chuck, I'm warned. No woman in her right mind would want a big ugly redhead for a husband, anyway. Think of what horrors they'd be if we had daughters."

"I'm willing to volunteer as a lover."

"I'll think about it. For tonight, Chuck, I need somebody to lean on, and those shoulders of yours look mighty reassuring. This damn blackout! Would you believe that a hip girl like me is afraid of the dark?"

She said it mockingly. But he caught something real underneath.

He touched her hand. "Lean all you want. By the way, what happened with your more-or-less fiancé?"

He turned out to be more less than more. I caught him with another dame."

"I should have been born Irish," Baer said. "I've got their luck. You want to dance some more? I liked that sample. Especially the part where I get to hold you in my arms."

Another piece had started. Turnboldt and the Hitchey girl were going at it again; Jeff Ring and the plump Benson girl moved onto the floor; Sybil Graves, who had been dancing with Corrigan, perched on the railing while Corrigan went to get her a drink.

"Not particularly," Sally said; but she put down her drink and held out her arms again.

They joined the dancers for a few turns, in silence.

"You don't really want to dance," Sally said suddenly.

"Not to dance," Baer confessed. "Just to hold you in my arms."

"We can't very well do that here without dancing," she murmured.

"Check. So let's go somewhere where we can."

For a long moment she said nothing, as if she were weighing certain imponderables. Then she looked up at him.

"All right. There's my studio." Then she stopped and said in dismay, "But it'll be dark."

"I thought I reminded you of the Rock of Gibraltar."

"All right," she said again. "All right."

She let him take her through the gate into the office hallway. The candlelight from the reception room died out quickly. By the time they reached the door at the end of the hall the girl was only a shadow to Baer. He opened the door, drew her inside, and closed it behind them.

It was not entirely dark in the studio. Moonlight streamed in through the three windows. Baer could make out easels, a work table, and against one wall a studio couch.

"We should have brought a candle," Sally said in a small voice. "Do you carry a lighter or something, Chuck?"

"It's out of juice."

"My purse is in here somewhere. There's a lighter in it."

She started for the work table. Baer caught her by one arm, swung her around, and took her by the shoulders.

"I can see well enough for what we have in mind," he said.

She looked up at him. When he dropped his hands to her waist, her arms came up immediately.

The intensity of the kiss left them both shaking. Sally said huskily, "I don't know what's got into me, Chuck. I've never in my life thrown myself like this at a man I just met . . ."

"Why worry about it?" Baer said, and led her over to the couch. He encountered no resistance whatever, not even a token. And yet, he told himself, this girl is no tramp. She seemed to have abandoned herself to the moment. It's the black-out, all right, he thought.

He laid her gently down on the couch and knelt on the floor beside her. He had unsnapped her brassiere and was pushing her dress and slip up when the door burst open and candlelight suddenly invaded the room. Baer jumped to his feet. Sally made a desperate grab for her brassiere and

121

sat up, pulling at her dress with the other hand.

Baer growled, "Didn't your mother teach you to knock, Turnboldt?"

The copywriter carried the candle over to the work table and slammed it down, glaring at Sally. "Can't you let one stud turn cold before you bed down with another? You hardly know this guy, you slut!"

Baer was a blur. One moment he was standing at the couch, the next his left fist described a four-inch arc and crashed into Turnboldt's chin. The copywriter's eyes crossed in the candlelight; he pitched forward and down as if he had been struck by a wrecker's ball. Baer caught him as he fell and lowered him gently to the floor, where he lay quite still, face down.

"That'll teach him manners," Baer said. "You all right, Sally?"

Sally was staring down at Turnboldt with shame, outrage, and amazement. Baer's lunge, his blow, had come so quickly that she was almost unable to accept it as an accomplished fact.

"What do you carry in that fist?" she said in a stifled voice; she was still smoothing her dress. "Grenades?"

"Don't worry, he won't suffer any permanent damage," Baer assured her. "Maybe a sore head for a while from the lump. He asked for it, Sally. I thought you said you didn't have a boy friend. This character acted mighty possessive to me."

"Tony isn't my boy friend," she flashed at him. "He's got a wife."

"Then what's his beef?"

"He's the married man I mentioned who's been making a play for me since I broke off my more-or-less engagement. I used to date him when he and his wife were separated, but he decided to go back to her. He tried to get me to keep going out with him, but that was it as far as I was concerned. I blasted him for suggesting it, and he was behaving himself toward me until very recently, when he started all over again, trying to warm up our romance. This thing just now is too much. I'll fix Mr. Turnboldt's wagon when he sobers up."

The redhead studied her. "What was that crack about your last stud not being cold yet?"

"He meant Brian Frank," she said with contempt. "He's the man I just threw over. But I wrote finis to that one long before Brian blew his brains out."

Baer glanced down at the unconscious Turnboldt. "He'll be coming to pretty soon. Anywhere else we can go, Sally?"

"Not now," Sally said. "He might just as well have thrown a pail of ice water at me. What are you made of, Chuck—lava?"

"Sex isn't one of my problems," he said, and shrugged. "Too bad—I was looking forward to it. Some other time, maybe."

"Maybe." She took her purse from the work table and picked up Turnboldt's candle. "I'll need this to go to the ladies' room and make repairs. Meet you back in the outer office."

Sally went out. Baer stooped over the prone copywriter in the moonlight and listened to his breathing. It was regular. He went back to the party, leaving Mr. Turnboldt to come to in solitary decency.

The radio was still playing, but no one was dancing. Ring, Eva Benson, and the Hitchey siren were crowded around the bar, where Ring was mixing drinks for them. Apparently Howard Craft had just replenished Laverne Thomas's cup and his own; he was standing before the sofa handing a cup to her. He reseated himself as Baer drifted by.

Tim and Sybil Graves weren't in the room, he noticed. Baer pushed through the gate and went over to the two uniformed men.

"Where's the captain?"

Coats, the younger cop, said, "He and Miss Graves stepped out a few minutes ago."

The Coleman lantern was still sitting on the railing, so Baer knew that the only light Corrigan had with him was his pencil flash. Maybe Tim was doing a little romancing himself. He decided not to go looking for him.

Just then Corrigan came in from the public hall, alone.

13.

Corrigan joined Baer at the desk where the two officers were seated.

"What happened to your suspect?" Baer grinned.

"Same thing that happened to yours," Corrigan retorted. "We ran into Sally Peterson in the hall, carrying a candle and heading for the john. Sybil decided to go with her."

So it's Sybil now instead of Miss Graves, Baer thought. He glanced at Corrigan's strong jaw and decided not to kid him about it.

Corrigan was looking around the room. "Where's Tony Turnboldt?"

"Sleeping it off in Sally's studio," Baer said.

Corrigan nodded. "He wasn't that potted. You slugged him?"

The redhead nodded. "He got a bit out of hand. Seems he and Sally made music one time. He was gassed enough to forget it was ancient history."

"So you sent him bye-bye when he caught you

with her pants down."

"It hadn't got to that. He called her a crude name. He ought to be staggering out any minute now."

Turnboldt appeared from the office hallway. He walked unsteadily and was feeling his jaw. As he pushed through the gate in the railing he murdered Chuck Baer with a glance. But that was all—he made for the bar and poured a stiff Scotch for himself.

Corrigan said reflectively, "Soon as Sybil and your artist gal get back, I'm going to stir things up a bit."

Baer elevated his thick red brows, but he asked no questions. He knew what Tim had in mind; they operated on psychic radar.

When Sally and Sybil came back, Turnboldt was dancing savagely with Wanda Hitchey, and Jeff Ring with the Benson girl. Turnboldt had maneuvered the sultry file clerk to the farthest corner, where the candlelight was dimmest.

Corrigan hoisted the gasoline lantern, set it on the desk at which the two cops sat, and pumped air. Young Coats struck a match for him. The MOS man spun the needle lever once to clear the gas line and nodded to Coats. The young officer pushed the match into the ignition hole, Corrigan opened the valve slightly, waited until the flame settled down, then opened the valve wide.

Light flooded the room; Wanda Hitchey looked startled and unglued herself from Turnboldt. The copywriter glared at Corrigan; his mouth was smeared with lipstick.

"What's the idea?" Turnboldt snarled. "What are you, light-crazy or something?"

"Hey," his pudgy co-writer protested. He was still dancing with the Adams receptionist. "Who needs it?"

Corrigan walked over and snapped the radio off. Sally Peterson, Sybil Graves, the couple on the sofa were all staring at him.

"Sorry to be a kill-joy," Corrigan said. "But I've let this act go on long enough. It's back to work, folks—real work."

"What do you mean?" Ring demanded. "I thought you'd finished with all that jazz."

"Hardly, Mr. Ring. You see, I still haven't found out which one of you murdered Brian Frank."

There was a ghastly silence.

"Murdered?" Sally Peterson said. *"Murdered?"*

"It couldn't have been an accident and it couldn't have been a suicide, Miss Peterson," Corrigan said. "But there he is across the hall with a hole in his temple and half his face blown off. What would you call it?"

The artist groped for a chair and remained standing. He saw incomprehension on every face, including Sybil's. Somebody, he thought, is one hell of an actor.

"But how could he possibly have been murdered, Captain Corrigan?" Laverne Thomas asked on a very high note. "It's ridiculous! Nobody but Mr. Frank was in that room. Unless—" She stopped short and stared at Sybil Graves.

The Irish complexion darkened; the blue eyes

went wide, then narrow.

"Unless I lied, you mean, Laverne? Unless I killed him?"

"I didn't say that," the spinster stuttered. "I mean—"

"Look," Corrigan said. "You all know there's a two-foot ledge runs clean around the twenty-first floor. According to Miss Graves, she didn't go immediately into Frank's office when she heard the shot. If that's true, the killer got in by way of that ledge and had enough time to make his escape the same way. So it could have been any one of you."

He let it sink in, avoiding Chuck Baer's glance. He was almost grateful when the timid brown eyes behind Howard Craft's bifocals blinked nervously and Craft protested, "I don't understand, Captain. What made you decide all of a sudden that Brian was murdered?"

"It wasn't all of a sudden," Corrigan told the jeweler. "I knew it the minute I took a look."

No one said anything, and Corrigan made them stew. It was Sally Peterson who finally asked, "What told you, Captain?"

"The safety on the P38 is set." Corrigan threw a deliberately amused look at Tony Turnboldt. "Frank's killer must have set it instinctively after firing the shot. It would have been impossible for Frank to have set it. He was dead."

It seemed to be sitting-down time. Turnboldt sank into the chair behind the nearest desk, mouth slightly open. Little Mrs. Benson flopped at her receptionist's desk, looking sick. Wanda Hitchey felt for the chair to one side of Eva Benson, Sybil Graves the one to the other side. Jeffrey Ring seemed to collapse against the desk where Turnboldt had sat down; he leaned there, breathing heavily. Sally Peterson waded through the gate as if it were surf and sought the safety of one of the overstuffed chairs in the reception area; Baer followed her through and perched on an arm, looking down at her. Howard Craft and Laverne Thomas simply sat where they were, on the sofa; only their eyes moved, in little sidewise jerks, as if seeking a point of exit.

So Corrigan was the only one left on his feet, which suited him fine. It added altitude to his mastery of the situation.

He said, in the driest voice he could command, "Anybody care to comment? The floor is open, ladies and gentlemen."

The alcoholic flavor had gone out of Turnboldt's voice; Corrigan's announcement had apparently sobered him up. "Anybody maneuvering on that ledge from this direction, Captain, would have had to pass my and Jeff's windows. It seems to me I'd have to have noticed if someone had passed those windows. And the only people who were still on the floor who could have come from the other direction were Howie and Laverne, and they alibi each other, don't they? That means the killer couldn't have used the ledge. And that leaves only one way the killer could have got into Brian's office—through the door from the Burns

Accounting reception room."

"Where I was!" Sybil flashed. "Why don't you go ahead and say it, Tony?"

"I'm not accusing anybody," the copywriter said; his eyes, usually bold, were evasive. "I'm just pointing out the facts."

"You've left a couple out, Mr. Turnboldt," Corrigan said, unmoved. "One: If you were hard at work at your desk in there, as you claim, you'd hardly have been watching windows. Two: Your analysis is based on the assumption that you were in your office. Now to me that's not necessarily the fact. You could be lying. In fact, you would naturally lie—if you were the one who stepped out on that ledge and headed for Brian Frank's window."

"I didn't! I'm telling the truth!"

"And you forgot one other point, Mr. Turnboldt. You could be telling the truth, and Miss Graves could be, too. It could have been done by someone stepping onto the ledge from the window at the rear of the public hall, between the two rest rooms."

Sally Peterson said in her metallic voice, "That would narrow it down to me and Wanda, wouldn't it, Captain?"

"I wish it were that simple, Miss Peterson. Unfortunately, the dead man's co-worker, Gil Stoner, could have sneaked back after ostensibly leaving for the day, and used that hall window. He seems to have had a pretty good motive. Theoretically, so could Mr. Burns and old Mr. Griswald.

Unless we dig up motives for Burns and Griswald, neither can be considered a live prospect for an arrest; we'll follow that up, though, as soon as we can, if only to rule them out. The likeliest suspect, aside from you people, is Stoner."

"Aren't you being awfully free with information, Captain?" Sally Peterson asked suddenly. "I've always understood that police officers keep their findings and theories pretty much to themselves until they're ready to jump. Especially to a bunch of suspects in a murder case. Are you sure you're an officer of the law? I don't remember, now that I think of it, your showing us your credentials."

"Glad to oblige," Corrigan said, and flashed his shield. He even smiled at her. "You're a smart girl, Miss Peterson. Of course you're right about the usual police methods. But the circumstances in this case aren't usual. One unique factor is the blackout. We don't know how long we'll have to be here. I'm on my own for the duration, and I'll conduct this case as I see fit. I see fit to lay my cards on the table; I advise you all to do the same. I have no preconceptions or prejudices about anybody involved; I'm simply trying to get at all the facts. Are we through talking about me?"

She did not answer; neither did anyone else.

"Good. Then we can start talking about you."

"Me?" the blonde artist said involuntarily.

"For openers. It looks as if you had both opportunity and possible motive. About motive— I understand you broke off a hot romance with the

131

late Mr. Frank only a short time ago?"

"I broke off with him, yes," Sally Peterson snapped. "If every bed-down that went sour in this town ended in the woman's blasting the head off the man, you'd have to quadruple the manpower in the police department. I didn't really give much of a damn about Brian. Ships that pass in the night, and so forth. There's always another man. So I didn't shoot him, Captain; you're wasting your time on me. Why don't you investigate Brian's stormier recent breakup? Like with Wanda Hitchey."

Corrigan already knew about that. He glanced at the over-cosmeticized file clerk with the belly-dancer build. "Any comment, Miss Hitchey?"

"You would, you bottle-blonde broad," Miss Hitchey said vindictively to the Peterson girl. "Captain, I'd be scared to pick up a gun, let alone shoot anybody with it. I've never touched one in my life. I don't operate like those girls in the tabs you're always reading about. I might give a two-timer a piece of my mind, or throw a staple machine at him, but how can you make up with a man when you've shot him dead? I'm the making-up kind."

Sally spat something, Wanda spat something back, and Corrigan turned his back on both of them. "I'm especially interested in you, Turnboldt." He deliberately left off the "Mr." this time. "You had opportunity, but if you had motive, I haven't uncovered it. It's hard for me to believe that two studs like you and Frank on this floor didn't tangle. I don't suppose you'll open up about it, but maybe somebody else will, if only to spread the wealth. How about it, somebody?''

"Somebody" turned out to be the plump little receptionist, Eva Benson. Corrigan was not surprised. The nice, retiring little ones often proved gold mines of information.

"Aren't you going to tell him about your run-in with Brian, Tony?''

The copywriter glowered at her. Mrs. Benson elevated her Dutch-maid shoulders.

"I didn't know what it was all about, Captain Corrigan, but Brian Frank punched Tony on the jaw and knocked him down a couple of weeks ago. It happened outside the men's room. Everybody here either saw it or heard the fight.''

"I'll tell you what it was all about," Sally Peterson said in an arctic voice. "It was Tony who told me about Brian and Wanda. He got floored for not minding his own business.''

Turnboldt shouted, "Big thanks I get for doing you a favor!''

"Favor, my eye. You broke up Brian and me because you hoped it would get you back in his place. I don't owe you anything but payment in kind for that, buster. And if I forgot to mention it, the next time you ask me for even the time of day I'm going to use my knee on you.''

Turnboldt's face turned lobster red. He half-raised himself out of his chair, as though to spring and destroy. But when he saw Chuck Baer's eyes concentrating on the purple lump on his jaw, he sank back.

Wanda Hitchey was examining Turnboldt in turn. "*You* snitched on Brian and me, Tony?"

There was no animosity in her tone. Turnboldt ignored her. He sucked on his handsome lower lip, deciding to ignore everybody.

"You did me a favor," Wanda said. "You made Sally throw Brian right in my lap. Well, it didn't last very long, and now he's gone forever."

And with this declaration of philosophy, Miss Hitchey turned to a critical survey of her fingernails.

It's a sad world, Corrigan thought. What two-legged bums the human race is, including, he thought, me.

"Of course, you're included as a suspect—Miss Graves." He had almost said "Sybil." "Although only from the standpoint of opportunity." He had to steel himself to keep his tone impersonal and his eye uninvolved. "I don't know of any motive." He faced them all with an effort they did not see. "Does anyone here know of a possible reason why Miss Graves might have wanted to kill Brian Frank?"

No one answered. It was not, he thought with relief, because of any delicacy of feeling or desire to protect the girl from across the hall. Not this bunch. If they didn't talk, it was because they knew of nothing to tell him.

Sybil said in a voice more frigid than Sally Peterson's had been, "You could have asked me, Captain. There was no relationship between Brian and me except strictly office. I suppose you'll ask

Gil Stoner and Mr. Burns when you get the chance, but they'll tell you the same thing."

So now I'm Captain again, Corrigan thought. Damn it! She didn't appreciate being a suspect in a murder case. Well, he thought, who would? It was a hell of a way to start a romance.

14.

Corrigan ran his eye around the room. "Now that you all know this is murder, anyone want to change his story?"

He expected no answer and he got none. He looked at Jeff Ring and little Mrs. Benson.

"Still alibi each other?"

The Dutch dairymaid said, "We told the truth, Captain."

Ring nodded anxiously.

Corrigan turned suddenly to the ill-fitting pair on the sofa. "How about you, Mr. Craft?"

"We told the truth," Howard Craft said with a start.

The aging secretary-bookkeeper was unruffled. "We were together when it happened, Captain. But there is one thing."

"What's that, Miss Thomas?"

"Ever since I learned that the gun used was Mr. Griswald's, I've been assuming Mr. Frank stole it from Mr. Griswald's desk yesterday morning, when he was making a stock inventory. He was around all morning, you see. But it couldn't have been Mr. Frank who stole it, could it?"

"No," Corrigan said. "It has to have been his killer."

"And it wasn't necessarily in the last few days that it was stolen?"

Corrigan was puzzled. "We may be able to narrow the time after we talk to Mr. Griswald and find out when he last checked to see if it was still in his desk. At this point we have to assume the killer could have lifted it at any time since the attempted holdup."

She took a sip from the plastic cup in her hand and gazed into space.

Corrigan said, "I don't quite see what you're getting at, Miss Thomas."

Her remoteness vanished. "Oh, I was trying to remember something." She giggled.

With a mild shock Corrigan realized that the gray-haired bookkeeper was tight. It shouldn't have surprised him; she had been accepting every drink handed to her since the odd party began. It was almost funny—like finding a pious maiden aunt sozzled on sacramental wine.

"Remember something about what, Miss Thomas?"

She was trying with dignity to focus. "Something sticks in my mind about somebody else having been around our office recently. But I can't seem to remember who or when. If that's what it is. I'm not even sure about that."

"You mean somebody who wouldn't ordinarily

be there?"

Laverne Thomas frowned into space again. Corrigan let her think. Finally she made a pawing little gesture.

"I don't know that I'd put it just *that* way, Captain. I mean, people come in and out all the time, so who's ordinary and who isn't? I *do* remember being surprised by whoever it was, but *why?*"

"A customer?"

She pursed her lips. "I don't know."

"Someone from this floor? Someone here now?"

Miss Thomas carefully surveyed the circle of faces. But she shook her head.

"It won't come, Captain. It's like a name you can't quite remember that keeps hanging on the tip of your tongue."

Her tongue was rapidly thickening. In her fogged condition she wasn't likely to recall anything tonight.

"Don't try to push it, Miss Thomas. Relax and forget about it. Maybe it will come later on."

The secretary-bookkeeper of Griswald Jewelers leaned forward to set her empty cup on the cocktail table before the sofa. Then she struggled to her feet and stood there swaying slightly.

"I have to go to the little girl's room," she announced, and giggled again.

"I think I'll go, too," Sally Peterson said, jumping up. "Eva, let me borrow your candle." She accepted the candle, took Laverne Thomas's elbow firmly, and steered her toward the door. "Excuse us," Sally said. "We'll be right back."

138

"Imagine," little Mrs. Benson said. "Miss Thomas pie-eyed."

"Big deal," Tony Turnboldt muttered, and relapsed into his surly, worried silence.

Corrigan looked around once more. "Does anyone have anything to say to me that hasn't already come out?"

No one did.

"Then there's nothing more I can do until the power comes back on and I can get police technicians up here." He waved. "Go back to your partying."

But the knowledge that what had been presumed suicide had been murder al¹ along sabotaged the party spirit. Inevitably they would be wondering which among them was a killer; it was hard to maintain a festive mood when you might wind up like the stiffening accountant across the hall. During the next hour or so Corrigan caught snatches of talk; there seemed to be general agreement that the absent Gil Stoner must be the bad guy. The psychology of their choice was obvious. It was easier on the nerves to assume that the killer was not one of them in their enforced and timeless imprisonment.

While Sally and Laverne Thomas were gone, Jeff Ring took over the bar, soliciting orders; no one switched the radio back on. Even Wanda Hitchey seemed no longer in the mood for dancing.

Sally and Miss Thomas came back from the ladies' room. The older woman was leaning heavily on the blonde's arm. Sally eased her to the sofa, where she leaned back and promptly shut her eyes. Sally reclaimed the easy chair, and Chuck Baer, who had refused Ring's offer of another drink, went over to the bar at Sally's request to make her one.

Sybil, Corrigan noticed, did not rejoin the others in drinking. He went over to her.

"Don't you want a drink, Sybil? I'll be glad to get you one." Glad was not exactly the word, but it was a way of re-establishing contact.

"No, thanks, Captain."

Corrigan smiled down at her. "I'm in the doghouse, I see."

She pretended not to understand. "What would I have to do with that?"

He felt a surge of irritation; he knew where it came from, but for some reason he didn't care. He could not recall the last time he had lost his cool during an investigation. "Come off it, Miss Graves! I'm already guilty of rotten police work where you're concerned. An officer has to lay aside his personal feelings on a case or he'd better hand in his shield."

"I don't know what you're talking about, Captain," Sybil said with a toss of her pert head.

"Don't you, now! You're giving me the treatment because I dared suggest you had opportunity to commit this crime. Among a lot of others, by the way. You're taking advantage of me. You know I'm interested in you—"

"Are you?" She flashed him that enchanting Irish smile. "Now how would I be knowin' that, Captain? Unless you tell me."

140

"I've told you," he said roughly.

"So you have. And you know something? I can hear the Killarney when you get mad—Tim."

He found himself smiling down at her again. "That's better."

"But you still consider me a suspect."

"I have to, Sybil. I have to."

"Sure, and you do that. I'm sorry, Tim. Of course. But I'm not worried, really. I didn't do it. I know that, and you'll know it as well as feel it before the night's over. I feel *that* in my bones."

She was a little witch. That was exactly it. "Drink?" he said.

She shook her head. "I do think I've had enough, Tim. Why don't we just sit and talk?"

"All right. But I'd better conserve fuel and turn the lantern off again."

With the room illuminated only by candlelight, the unhappy company drifted by instinct into pairing off again. Wanda Hitchey moved over to her own desk, where Turnboldt was seated, and sat down beside it. Jeff Ring seated himself beside the reception desk in the chair vacated by Wanda. Chuck Baer remained on the arm of Sally Peterson's chair; and Howard Craft hitched a little closer to Laverne Thomas on the sofa. She was snoring.

Corrigan pulled a chair over to Sybil.

She said, "I'm curious about your eye, Tim. Unless you'd rather not discuss it."

"It was a shell fragment. Korea. I still have the chunk. It's in a cabinet in my apartment."

She made a face. "That's gruesome."

141

He shook his head. "I never think of it that way. It's just a souvenir of the war. Incidentally, that redheaded ox over there dragged me to the aid station."

Sybil glanced over at Chuck Baer. He was leaning over, whispering something to Sally. The blonde smiled and shook her head.

"Your hero just got a no answer in a proposition," Sybil said. "I take it you're old friends."

"None older."

She asked him about his background and revealed her own. She had come to New York from Iowa seven years ago, at the age of twenty-one. She had managed to earn two years of college credit in business administration at N.Y.U. night school while holding down a job. Until a few months ago she had been private secretary to an insurance broker; she had lost her job when he retired.

"I may be in the same spot at Burns before long. Mr. Burns is sixty-seven. He's talking about retiring, too. This horrible thing tonight may jolt him into the decision."

At regular intervals Turnboldt or Ring would get up and visit the bar to refill their cups; the others, including the girls they had paired off with, had apparently decided they had had enough. From scraps of conversation between Ring and little Mrs. Benson, sitting within earshot, the fattening copywriter was already halfseas over. Turnboldt and the Hitchey girl were too far away to be overheard, but from the way he walked and the glaze in his eyes he was obviously in the same condition.

142

While he was not deliberately eavesdropping on Ring and Eva Benson, Corrigan could not help overhearing most of what they said; their talk formed a sort of counterpoint to his own dialogue with Sybil. The early part of their talk consisted largely of an effort to convince each other that the absent Gil Stoner must be Frank's killer. Then, as Ring got drunker, he began to get romantic.

Ring was apparently one of those chronically married men who keep their noses clean all year but cut loose at the annual office party and start chasing the stenos. He was transparent enough; the murder, the blackout, the enforced isolation of the people in the office had triggered the Christmas psychology. Corrigan was more interested in little Mrs. Benson. She could not be more than twenty-four or so; she could not have worn that cheap wedding band for very long. Cut off from her husband with no certainty about when she could rejoin him, the eerie atmosphere of the blacked-out city beyond the windows, the liquor she had drunk—would she encourage old Jeff? Corrigan thought he saw her hesitate, speculate. But when Ring began to paw her, he saw her stiffen and draw back.

"Look, Jeff," he heard her say. "You're a nice guy and all that, but no hands, please. That's off limits to everybody but my husband. Incidentally, he's twenty years younger than you and he looks like Tony Curtis. If I seemed to be encouraging you when we were dancing, I'm sorry. It must have been the liquor. Okay?"

Jeff Ring had looked positively comical.

Corrigan saw him glance down at his potbelly and begin to shake. He muttered something, got up, went back to the bar, and downed a stiff slug. When he reeled back, he sat heavily down and began to sing a sad song. There was pity in young Mrs. Benson's eyes; she reached over and patted his hand. It seemed to buck him up, and they began to talk about the blackout.

15.

Corrigan did not realize how much time had passed until Sybil suddenly shivered.

"You know it's getting cold in here?"

He leaned toward Eva Benson's desk to examine his watch by the candlelight. It was almost ten-thirty. He got up and went over to feel the radiator. It was cold.

The building must have a thermostatically controlled furnace that had kicked off when the power failed. The water from the boiler circulating through the heating system would take several hours to cool off. It was long past that point.

He returned to Sybil. "With the windows closed, it should stay tolerable. It's chilly out, but not really cold. How far away do you live, Sybil?"

"Too far to walk."

"Then you're planning to sleep here tonight?"

"I guess we'll all have to. Mr. Burns has a nice soft rug in his office. I'll stretch out on that and use my coat for a blanket."

Eva Benson overheard. "I'm about ready to call it a night, too, Sybil." She called over to Howard Craft, "You and Laverne are on what I intend to use for a bed, Howie. You'll have to find somewhere else to roost soon."

Craft immediately rose, leaned over Laverne, and shook her. The woman blinked up at him. She mumbled something and promptly went back to sleep.

Sally Peterson said, "Give Howie a hand with her, Chuck."

Baer went over to the sleeping bookkeeper and picked her up as effortlessly as if she had been an infant. The woman's eyes popped open; for an instant she stared, terrified, into Baer's face. Then she looked pleased, shut her eyes again, and contentedly dropped her gray head to his shoulder.

"Where do you want Sleeping Beauty?" Baer asked Craft.

"In her own office, I suppose," the jeweler said. "There's a rug on the floor there, Mr. Baer. I'll get a candle."

He pushed through the swinging gate and went over to the bar for the candle burning there. Wanda Hitchey called, "Light a fresh one, Howie. If we're going to bed down in separate offices, we'll need all the candles there are."

The three unused candles lay on the table. Craft held one to the flame, emptied the butts from an ashtray into a wastebasket, dripped wax into the tray, and fixed the base of the candle in the melted wax.

As Craft brought the candle back through the gate, Laverne Thomas's left eye opened to a slit and sneaked a quick look up into Baer's face. Sally Peterson got out of her chair and peered at the gray-haired woman. Miss Thomas promptly squeezed her eyes shut.

"She's playing possum!" Sally exclaimed. "How do you like that?"

Baer grinned and nodded to Craft to precede him with the candle.

"I think I'll chaperone this trip," Sally said, "to make sure Laverne doesn't enjoy it too much."

She trailed the two men and Baer's burden out into the public hall.

Ring muttered to Eva Benson, "If you're taking the sofa, Eva, mind if I use the easy chair?"

"I don't own this office," the little receptionist said. "Sleep where you want, Jeff."

And Wanda Hitchey said, "Before anybody else lays claim to it, I'm staking out the divan in the powder room."

In a thick voice Tony Turnboldt said, "I'll share it with you, baby."

"In the powder room?" Wanda seemed horrified. "I should say not!"

Turnboldt leered. "Can't blame a guy for trying. I guess I'll have to stretch out on the desk in my office."

Chuck Baer and Sally Peterson came back without the candle.

"Laverne's tucked in," Baer said with a grin. "We left the candle near her on the floor."

147

"She's absolutely *wide* awake," Sally said. "Who'd have thought it of that old biddy? Making believe she'd passed out just so she could nestle in Chuck's manly arms!" She looked at Baer affectionately. "For a guy as ugly as you are, Chuck, you sure have a way with women."

"Especially the old babes," Baer said. "And dogs and drooly kids."

"We'll take up a benefit for you," Corrigan said. "Where's Craft bedding down?"

"In Uncle Everett's office."

"Who?"

"Old man Griswald. Howie's uncle."

"Craft has no candle."

"He doesn't need one. There's plenty of moonlight coming in."

Sally picked up from the reception desk the stub of candle that had originally lighted up the office. She ignited it from the flame of the newer candle on the desk.

"Me, I'm retiring to my studio," she said, and glanced at Baer.

He fell in by her side. "I'll tuck you in," he said. They went up the office hall. That takes care of Chuck for the night, Corrigan thought enviously. He could never get over Baer's magical effect on certain women.

Wanda Hitchey retrieved her heavy cloth coat from the closet. "I'm retiring to my boudoir in the ladies' room," she announced. "Night, all."

"Wait." Turnboldt gripped the edge of the desk and pulled himself to his feet with obvious difficulty. "Long's everybody's tucking everybody in, might's well tuck you in, Wanda."

Wanda's green eyes appraised his condition. She draped her coat over the chair he had vacated and took him by the elbow.

"You'd never make it back down the hall," she said. "I'll tuck *you* in, Tony." She steered him over to the door leading to the copywriters' office in the northwest corner of the floor. He kept lurching against her. But Corrigan noticed that when they got to the door it was Turnboldt who reached for the knob and twisted it. He did it without fumbling. The couple disappeared through the doorway. Turnboldt wasn't half as drunk as he was making out. Corrigan wondered why. Maybe it was a ploy to lure Wanda into thinking he was incapable of making a pass. Not that Wanda seemed in need of luring.

At that moment Wanda reappeared, without the candle. She went over to the closet, got a man's topcoat out of it, and went back into Turnboldt's office.

The two hapless police officers came over to Corrigan. "How about us, Captain?" asked Maloney, the older one.

"Why not call in now instead of waiting until eleven-thirty?" Corrigan suggested. "It doesn't look as if we'll get power back tonight any more."

Maloney went over to the phone and dialed. He dialed again. The third time he dialed Operator. After a long wait he got her, listened, and hung up glumly. "Every line is tied up, Captain. Everybody

149

stuck in town is apparently trying to call home. I tell you it's like the end of the world. Can't make a simple call!"

"Where do we flop, Captain?" asked the younger officer.

"We have to have a guard on the murder room, so it'll have to be across the hall at Burns Accounting. Miss Graves is sleeping in Mr. Burns's private office, though, and I am planning to use her desk in the reception room. There's nothing else to sleep on in that outer office but bare floor."

Young Coats looked startled. "You mean we have to sleep in that room with the dead man, sir?"

"It's not an order, Coats," Corrigan said, keeping a straight face. "But it has a carpeted floor. Just a suggestion. If you can't stomach it, stretch out on the floor of the outer office, or sleep in a chair."

Maloney said to his young partner, "You do that, Coats. I've seen my share of stiffs. I don't mind stretching out on the carpet with the dead man."

"Just don't disturb the evidence, Maloney," Corrigan said.

Coats hastily went over to pump up the lantern and light it.

Wanda Hitchey had come out of Turnboldt's office again and shut the door behind her. Apparently she had left the candle for Turnboldt, because she was now carrying the flashlight Turnboldt had stuffed into his topcoat pocket.

The auburn-haired office siren picked up her coat, uttered a general sexy good night, snapped on the flash, and headed for the ladies' room.

Chuck Baer reappeared as young Coats got the lantern going. Apparently Sally Peterson had decided not to give in too easily. Smart girl! Baer loved them and left them. Corrigan gave the private detective a sympathetic wink and got a black scowl in reply.

"How about lending me that pencil flash of yours so I don't break my neck on those stairs?" Baer growled at him.

"You're going home, Chuck?"

"Sure. Party's over."

Silently Corrigan took the flash from his pocket and gave it to him.

"See you tomorrow," Baer said. He turned to the portly copywriter. "Thanks for the booze, Ring."

Jeff Ring barely nodded. He was having trouble keeping his eyes open. Baer grunted in disgust and walked out.

"Bring the lantern, Coats, and we'll stake out our flops," said Officer Maloney. "Is it okay, sir?"

Corrigan nodded. The two bluecoats left with the Coleman.

In the considerably darkened office, Ring suddenly decided he needed a nightcap. As he staggered to the bar, Eva Benson went to the closet and got out a ratty fur coat. She headed for the sofa in the reception area.

Corrigan picked up one of the unused candles, then went over to the reception desk for the candle burning there.

"We'll take this and leave you the one on the table," he said to the receptionist.

She nodded, kicked off her shoes, stretched out on the sofa, and pulled the fur coat over her.

As Corrigan left with Sybil Graves, he heard Mrs. Benson call out, "Don't you think you've had enough, Jeff? Blow out that candle. I want to sleep."

They crossed the hall to Sybil's office. The door to the death room stood open, and light from the Coleman lantern was spilling through. Corrigan set the burning candle and the unlit one on Sybil's desk and went over to look into the inner office.

The lantern stood on the table used by the murdered man's fellow-accountant, Gil Stoner. In one corner of the office, as far from the body as he could get, Officer Maloney was squatted, testing the softness of the carpet. Coats was standing near the doorway uncertainly.

"Decided to sleep in there after all?" Corrigan asked him, amused.

"That damn wood floor out there is too hard, Captain," young Coats said.

Corrigan returned to the desk. He lit the second candle from the flame of the first and fixed it to the desk ashtray with melted wax. Sybil had gone over to a locker and taken out her short coat. It looked more stylish than warm.

"That doesn't look like much of a blanket, Sybil. It's going to get cold in here tonight."

"It's all I have."

Chuck Baer's coat and hat were gone from the

table that held the business machines. But Corrigan's were still there, and he picked up his coat, took one of the two candles, and said, "After you, Miss Graves."

He preceded her to the door lettered CARLE-TON BURNS, PRESIDENT.

16.

Corrigan set the candle and coat down on Burns's desk. Sybil draped her coat over the back of a chair.

She glanced over at Corrigan's coat. "If you mean that for me, Tim, I'm not going to take it and let you freeze."

"I know where there's another one," he said.

She looked at him.

"Brian Frank must have worn one to work this morning. It must be in his locker. I thought you'd prefer mine to his."

He warmed to her smile. There was something about the dramatic dimness of the office, the black sky beyond the window, the general silence that had settled over the twenty-first floor, that made him tingle suddenly. He felt a familiar tickle in his groin. Whoa, boy!

"I didn't know cops could be sensitive. You're right, Tim. It's silly, but I couldn't possibly sleep under Brian's coat."

"Pick your bed and I'll snug you in." He looked

around. "Too bad your boss doesn't go for couches in his office."

She laughed. "He's too old."

"Pick your bed, colleen."

She chose the edge of the rug nearest the window. He fished the thick foam-rubber pad from Carleton Burns's swivel chair and laid it on the floor to serve as her pillow. She lay down, slipped off her shoes, and looked up at him. "Who says a rug is soft? I'm going to get up tomorrow morning feeling like a bag of broken bones."

He did not reply; for some reason he was finding it hard to talk. He draped her coat over her torso and his over her legs. Then he put something on the desk beside the candle.

"What's that, Tim?" she murmured.

"A pack of matches, in case you have to get up in the middle of the night."

He blew out the candle and went over to the window to adjust the Venetian blind, shutting out the moon. She stared up at him. The glow from the candle he had left burning on her desk in the outer office threw some faint light into the room. There was no longer any from the Coleman lantern. Either Coats had put it out or had shut the door of the death room.

"Good night, Tim." He could barely hear her.

"I haven't tucked you in yet."

It was an excuse to get near her again; he knew it, she knew it. Still, he was not conscious of any design. He knelt beside her and began to fumble with the coats. He was aware of the shimmer of her eyes; she seemed fascinated, as if he were a snake.

Maybe I am, he thought. Why am I doing this? What's got into me? Why this girl and not one of the others? It was not because she was Irish, too; at least he thought not; there was no chauvinism in him. . . . Her arms slid around his neck.

It took him totally by surprise. Up to this point he had been thinking of his own dark intentions; it had not occurred to him that this girl might be cozened by some outside force into taking an action she might under other circumstances control. The next thing Corrigan knew he was lying on the rug beside her; they were clinging to each other, kissing like lovers.

One time she pulled her face back for air; the grip of her arms about his neck did not relax. Her body against his was as taut as a high wire.

"Sleep here, Tim," she whispered. "With me."

He disengaged himself, found himself on his feet. He was aware of a vast turbulence in his head. "I'll be right back," he said.

He went into the reception room and blew out the candle. When he came back, he shut the door.

He took off his shoes in the darkness, slipped out of his coat, loosened his tie. When he got to her, feeling his way, she was holding up his side of the makeshift coverlet of coats. He slid under them, and they embraced.

It was while they were in the exploratory stage that Corrigan was struck by the curse of his profession. She's not a tart, his mind said, standing aside from his body and what it was doing; she never saw me before tonight; why is she giving in to me this way—so soon—with such initiative? Could this be an act? If so, why?

He had known the possible answer in the first lightning flash of the analysis: She had seen his instant interest in her, she was playing on it, she had a reason for wanting him emotionally involved with her, and the reason had been before his one eye from the start.

All that ledge business was a fantasy. No one had crawled along the ledge. It was the simplest of cases. She was the only one on the twenty-first floor who had had direct access to Brian Frank's office. She had gone from the outer office into the inner office and shot him. All the rest was out of a detective story.

She felt his withdrawal, of course.

"What's the matter, Tim?" she asked. There was trouble in her whisper. "Something's the matter."

I haven't a shred of evidence one way or the other, he thought desperately. It's just my damned training. She could be as innocent as the night is long.

"Nothing," Corrigan muttered; and at that moment the telephone in the outer office rang like a cockcrow.

"Answer it," Sybil said urgently. "Hurry, Tim, or one of those policemen in Brian's room will wake up."

He was on his feet, groping for Carleton Burns's desk and the packet of matches without conscious thought. As he grabbed them, the backwash of his gesture struck the candle and jarred loose the waxy seal holding it erect in the ashtray. He heard the candle roll off the desk and hit the rug with the softest sound.

By then the phone had rung three times. Corrigan sped across the room to the door, fumbled for the knob, found it, yanked, and shuffled quickly in the general direction of Sybil's desk. He felt for the phone and snatched it up, cutting it off in its sixth ring. At that moment the door to the accountants' room opened and young Coats stood there holding a flaming match.

"I've got it, Coats," Corrigan said. He said into the phone, "Hello?"

A female voice that sounded familiar said, "Is Captain Corrigan there?"

Coats came into the room. He shook out the match as it singed his fingers, struck another, and lit the candle on the desk.

"Speaking," Corrigan said. "Who's this?"

"Laverne Thomas, Captain. I'm down the hall in my office at Griswald Jewelers."

"Yes?" What was this, now?

"I phoned Adams Ad Agency first," the book-keeper said. "Mr. Ring answered and said you were spending the night at Burns. Did I disturb you?"

"What's the problem, Miss Thomas?"

"I've been lying here thinking. All of a sudden I realized what's been bothering me ever since Mr. Frank was murdered. It wasn't what I thought. Could you come over here, Captain?"

He was all alertness now. "You bet. It'll take me a couple of minutes; I'm half-dressed."

"Take your time, Captain. I'm not sleepy. You won't believe what I have to tell you. But I'm sure you can guess."

"You know who killed Brian Frank," Corrigan said abruptly.

"Yes."

"WHO?"

There was no answer. He said, "Hello, hello," realized that she had hung up, and slammed the receiver down.

Corrigan glanced at Coats. The young officer was fully dressed except for his overcoat and shoes. His eyes strayed toward the dark open doorway where Sybil lay waiting, then shifted hastily when he saw Corrigan watching him.

"Light your lantern, Coats," the MOS man said curtly. "I have some business down the hall."

From the doorway of the accountants' room, Officer Maloney said, blinking, "Something wrong, Captain?"

"Nothing that needs help. Go back to sleep, both of you."

He waited until Coats shut the door of the death room behind them, then hurried into Carleton Burns's office. By the candlelight from the outer office he could see Sybil on her feet, adjusting her clothing.

She seemed preoccupied and ashamed. Second thoughts? But he had no time for her now. Laverne Thomas's information might well wrap the case up. He had had a narrow escape; what he had done in Carleton Burns's office could cost him his shield. As it was, he was still in danger. Young Coats's glance at Burns's open doorway, the absence of any sign that Corrigan had been

159

stretched out in the reception room, could hardly have failed to tell him the story. He would have to rely on the young officer's discretion.

He put his shoes on swiftly, slipped on his jacket, tightened the knot of his tie. He was making the last adjustment when he heard the accountants' door open and saw the bright light of the Coleman lantern. He stepped out of Burns's office and shut the door.

"Just reassuring Miss Graves that everything was all right," Corrigan said. "I thought I told you to go back to sleep."

Coats said in a dutiful voice, "I thought you might want the lantern, sir."

"Oh. Thanks, Coats. Now I mean it. Go on back to sleep."

"Yes, sir."

He waited for Coats to leave. Then he blew out the candle on the desk and, bearing the Coleman, stepped out into the hall.

To his surprise he found the entrance to Griswald Jewelers unlocked. The display room was empty; the doors to the rooms to either side of it were closed.

He rapped on the unmarked door to the right, Laverne Thomas's office.

"Miss Thomas?"

There was no answer. She must have fallen asleep anyway, he thought, and opened the door.

Laverne Thomas lay on her back on the floor behind her desk. A candle on the desk was burning. A woman's cloth coat on the carpeted

160

floor at the far wall indicated where she had bedded down. A purse and a pair of walking shoes lay beside it.

The gray-haired woman's eyes were open, but she was not looking at anything. The leather-bound haft of what seemed to be a letter opener stuck up from between her flat breasts like a claim marker. There was very little blood.

Corrigan wasted no time. She was either dead or so far gone as to be beyond help. And there was no one else in the room.

He was out of the office and across the display room with its empty glass cases in a few bounds, to crash through the door into Everett Griswald's private office.

He held the Coleman lantern high.

Howard Craft lay wrapped in a dark blue chesterfield on the carpeted floor before the time vault, back to the door, his body curled in a prenatal posture. At the crash of the door and the invasion of the light he jerked upright, eyes slitted against the brightness; they began to blink. His mouth was half-open.

"What—" he began in a slurry voice.

Corrigan darted back through the display room to the hall door and diagonally across the hall to the unmarked door of Sally Peterson's studio. Only when the door yielded to his shove did he realize that it should have been on automatic lock; that it was not indicated a hope, perhaps, on the Peterson woman's part that Chuck Baer might be coming back. Or was it prearranged between them? Or . . . was it for some other reason?

The blonde was lying on her studio couch, a coat draped over the upper part of her body, a paint-spattered canvas tarp over her legs. Her sharp eyes popped open as he burst in.

"What the hell are you doing in my bedroom?"

She said it amiably, without belligerence. There was no one else in the studio.

Corrigan neither answered nor paused. He ran through the doorway into the agency hall, legged it up to the reception room, flashed the lantern around. Little Eva Benson lay curled on the sofa wrapped in her fur coat, sleeping like a child. Jeff Ring was sprawled in the easy chair nearby, feet on the cocktail table, topcoat pulled up to his neck, snoring.

Mrs. Benson's eyes opened; she sat up, terrified, clutching the coat to her. Ring merely shifted in the overstuffed chair, head cocked at a ludicrous angle, but Corrigan noticed that he stopped snoring; was he shamming? He had no time to speculate. He was through the gate in the railing and across the outer office to the door of the copywriters' office in four leaps.

Tony Turnboldt had shoved his and Ring's desks together and was lying across them catty-cornered, for greater length. He was using two chair cushions as a pillow and his topcoat as a blanket. He stirred at the opening door and the invasion of the Coleman.

Corrigan went to him and shook him roughly. Turnboldt's eyes flickered open. They immediately closed at the glare of the lantern.

"What the hell?" he muttered.

Corrigan set the lantern on the floor. He seized the man by the ankles and yanked. Turnboldt had to sit up to avoid being pulled to the floor. The topcoat slid off, and Corrigan saw that he was fully dressed except for his shoes. He had not even loosened his collar or tie.

"Whassa idea?" Turnboldt demanded, glaring.

"Rise and shine," Corrigan said. "We've had another homicide."

"Uh?" Turnboldt said. His mouth remained open. His eyes were streaked with blood. He had a heavy beard and it was beginning to show. He looked like a rummy.

Still, Corrigan wondered. The whole thing could be an act. He had drunk a lot, but what was his capacity? He could not get over the feeling that Turnboldt had not been half as plastered as he had seemed.

Corrigan ran out and across the outer room into the public hallway. He sped to the rear of the hall and pulled open the door of the ladies' room without hesitation.

Immediately inside there was a powder room; beyond it the lavatory and toilet facilities. There was a dressing table with a bench, and a divan against the opposite wall. Wanda Hitchey lay asleep on the divan under her coat.

Unless the man Stoner was still skulking around the building, that placed all possible suspects bedded down and apparently asleep

163

minutes after the second murder. Well, Corrigan thought, at least the magic number's been reduced by one. For this one Sybil Graves had a perfect alibi.

He could not have felt more relieved if she had been his mother.

17.

The Hitchey girl sat up and drew her coat around her as though Corrigan had caught her naked. She was all dressed except for her shoes.

"What are you, a sex fiend or something?" she cried. "This is the ladies' room!"

"Get up and go back to the Adams office," Corrigan said.

"Why should I?" She gave him the little-girl pout. Her lipstick was smeared, and she looked silly.

"Because I told you to. There's been another murder."

The door cut off her shriek.

Howard Craft appeared in the doorway of Griswald Jewelers at the other end of the hall. In a voice full of disbelief he called, "Captain, Laverne is in here—in here—I mean—"

"I know it," Corrigan said. "Go into 2103 with the others and wait for me."

He went back into 2101. The door into Carleton

Burns's office and the door into the accountants' room both stood open. The death room was dark, but Sybil had recovered her candle from the floor of the other and put one of his matches to it. By its light she was bent over tidying her hair and studying her face in the mirror of her compact, lying open on the desk.

When the lantern flooded the outer office with light, Sybil came running to the doorway.

"What was it, Tim?" she asked.

"Somebody just stuck a knife in Laverne Thomas."

He had answered without thinking. It was a technique, designed to shock suspects into a telltale reaction. But Sybil was no longer a suspect. Laverne Thomas had been about to give him the name of the killer of Brian Frank. She must have been right, or the killer was afraid that she might be. In either event, the one who shut the Thomas woman's mouth for good had to be the one who shot Frank to death. And since Sybil couldn't possibly have murdered Miss Thomas, she was eliminated as the murderer of Frank.

Sybil took it hard. Her blue eyes widened like a puddle in a sudden downpour; she actually shrank from him.

"I'm sorry, colleen," Corrigan said. "That was brutal."

"Poor, poor Laverne." It was all she could get out.

Maloney and Coats were just coming out of the accountants' room.

"Did we hear you right, Captain?" Maloney

asked anxiously. "Somebody attacked Miss Thomas with a knife?"

"Somebody killed Miss Thomas with a knife," Corrigan said. "I didn't stop to check her out, but nobody could survive with six inches of steel through her heart. Get your shoes on. We've got to start all over again."

In her confusion Sybil apparently took it as an order to her. She groped her way back in Carleton Burns's office; she came back out with her shoes, and put them on without sitting down.

They left 2101 in a body.

"Sybil," Corrigan said gently. "Join the others in the ad agency. We'll be along in a minute."

She gulped and obeyed. There was the slightest buzzing from 2103 as they passed the doorway. He caught a glimpse of white, staring faces; then he forgot them.

A thorough inspection of Laverne Thomas's office turned up nothing in the way of clues. The woman herself was already turning cold; Corrigan had been right. Without touching it, he took a close look at the leather hilt protruding from her chest. It was the haft of a letter opener, all right.

She had left no note. Not anything. She had expected Corrigan, and she had received a deadlier visitor.

He felt like cursing. Instead, he went out into the display room, wrapped his handkerchief around the phone, and dialed headquarters. All he got were busy signals.

"The hell with it," he said, replacing the phone. "All the rules are suspended tonight, anyway."

He led the way to the Adams Advertising Agency. Everyone was there, waiting.

Corrigan pushed through the gate and set the lantern on the railing. The two officers blocked the doorway.

"Who shot her?" Sally Peterson asked.

Smart? Corrigan wondered. The question adroitly disclaimed knowledge of how Laverne died.

"Didn't anyone tell you how Miss Thomas died?"

Apparently the same thought had occurred to Wanda Hitchey. "Laverne was stabbed, dear. As though you didn't know." She spat it.

Sally looked the file clerk over. "What's that supposed to mean?"

Corrigan said to the Hitchey girl, "How do you know she was stabbed?"

"Howie saw her. He says her own letter opener is sticking out of her chest."

Corrigan glanced at Howard Craft. "You recogized the murder weapon?"

"Yes," the jeweler said; his voice was still shaky. "I took a good look at her, hoping she might still be alive. She kept that paper knife on her desk."

So the weapon was meaningless as a clue, unless the killer had been kind enough to leave fingerprints on it. Corrigan had few hopes about the kindness of the killer.

He walked over to the railing and looked down at Jeff Ring.

"I spoke to Miss Thomas on the phone a few

minutes before she was stabbed. She said she phoned here first, Ring.''

The copywriter nodded; he seemed altogether sober. "It woke up Eva and me. I'd just gone back to sleep when you tore through here.''

"Me, too," the receptionist said.

Corrigan looked them over. "Neither of you left here after her phone call?''

Ring caught the implication first. "We're each other's alibis again, Captain.''

"Don't look at me," Tony Turnboldt snarled. "I was passed out.''

Corrigan said, "You seem to have made a remarkable recovery.''

"I just threw up out of my office window. Go take a look at the ledge if you don't believe me.''

Eva Benson said fearfully, "I'll bet Gil Stoner came back. I'll bet he's been hanging around the building all this time.''

"Don't be an idiot, Eva," Sally Peterson snapped. "We may as well face it. One of us has to be the killer. You and Jeff alibi each other for both murders, and Laverne alibied Howard Craft for the first one. That leaves me, Wanda, Tony, and Sybil holding the bag.''

Corrigan said smoothly, "Miss Graves was sleeping in her boss's office when I took the call from Laverne in the outer office. There's no door from Carleton Burns's office into the public hall—to get to the Griswald office she'd have had to pass me, and she didn't. Miss Graves is cleared.''

He thought young Coats gave him a funny look.

Sybil's was pure worship. Anyway, in essence it was true. She couldn't have done it.

Tony Turnboldt said to Wanda Hitchey in the same snarl, "Since I'm innocent, baby, that narrows it down to you and Sally."

"In a pig's eye it does! Who'd take your word for anything?" The girl was livid.

"Let's get back on the track," Corrigan said. "Ring, just what did you and Miss Thomas say to each other on the phone?"

"She asked if you were still here. I said no, she should phone Burns Accounting, because you'd said you planned to sleep there."

"Repeat the exact conversation. As nearly as you can remember it."

"Sure," the portly copywriter said quickly. "I picked up the phone and said, 'Adams Ad Agency.' Like you do. It could hardly be a business call at that time of night, but you get in the habit."

"I know. Go on."

"Laverne asked for you. I told her—"

"I want the exact words she used and your exact words in reply."

"She said, 'Mr. Ring? This is Laverne Thomas.' She always called everybody but Howie by the last name, though most of us called her Laverne. I said, 'Oh, it's you, Laverne.' Then—"

Corrigan interrupted again. "You said, 'Oh, it's you, *Laverne?*'"

Ring seemed puzzled. "I think that's what I said." He glanced at the receptionist. "Didn't I mention Laverne's name, Eva?"

170

She nodded with vigor.

So anyone overhearing Ring's side of the conversation would have known whom he was talking to. Corrigan said, "All right."

Ring said, "She asked, 'Is Captain Corrigan still there?' I said, 'No, Captain Corrigan is spending the night at Burns Accounting. Everybody's hit the sack.' She said, 'Thanks, Mr. Ring,' and hung up."

"You sure you mentioned me by name? Couldn't you have said, '*He's* spending the night over at Burns Accounting?'"

Ring looked sheepish. "I think those were my words, Captain." Again he appealed to Mrs. Benson.

"I know he mentioned your name, Captain," the girl said, "because when Jeff hung up I didn't have to ask him what the phone call had been about. I remember saying to him, 'I wonder what Laverne wants with Captain Corrigan all of a sudden?'"

Corrigan had what he had been probing for. Anyone overhearing the phone conversation would have known who the caller was and what she wanted. The ringing phone would have been heard both in Turnboldt's office and Sally Peterson's studio. Turnboldt could have eavesdropped by cracking open the door from his office. Sally could have come from her studio and up the hall far enough to overhear without being seen; the hall was pitch black. And both had been alone.

With the building quiet, even Wanda Hitchey

could have heard the ringing phone from the ladies' room. She could have pussyfooted up the hall and got an earful.

It was almost a dead certainty that the killer had overheard Laverne's call to Jeff Ring. He would have had time to get to Laverne's office door and eavesdrop on her call to Corrigan.

Opportunity was about equal for all three suspects. Sally Peterson could have faded back down the Adams hallway to her studio, then used the studio door into the public hallway, leaving the door unlocked for her return. Wanda, already in the public hall, could have reached Laverne's office even more quickly. Tony Turnboldt would have had to use the ledge to get from his office to the corridor, but it was only a few feet from his north window to the window at the rear of the hall; and from previous examination Corrigan knew that the hall window was not locked.

He should have placed more stock in Laverne's tipsy maunderings. Well, he hadn't, and she had paid for his omission with her life. He could not fault himself enough for his work on this case. Why hadn't he taken the poor woman seriously?

Someone had. Someone who didn't dare risk Laverne's telling him whatever it was.

Corrigan's cold voice told nothing of his thoughts. "Miss Thomas wanted to tell me who killed Brian Frank. Apparently she remembered some incident that told her who it had been." He glanced at Howard Craft. "You were closer to her than anyone here, Craft; you worked together. Do you have any idea what it might have been?"

Howie Craft's pinched, pale face waggled from side to side. "I'm afraid I don't—"

And then he stopped, appalled.

"What is it?" Corrigan asked quickly.

Craft said slowly, "Maybe I do know."

Corrigan felt a surge of relief. This could be it.

18.

The jewelry clerk said, "About a week ago—last Wednesday, it was—after Uncle Everett left for the day at his usual time, four-thirty, I went up the hall to the men's room. I wasn't gone more than five minutes. When I came back, I stuck my head in Laverne's office and she asked what I had been doing in my uncle's office. When I told her I hadn't been there, that I'd been in the men's room, she said she had looked out into the display room just in time to see the door into Uncle Everett's office close. It must have been while I was out, but since I wasn't in the display room she assumed it was me. Ordinarily she wouldn't have thought anything about it, since I'm in and out of there all day, except that I never shut myself in. I mean, if I go in for something when Uncle Everett isn't there, I leave the door open until I come out again. So it had bothered her that I had closed the door this time. When I told her it hadn't been me, we both went into Uncle Everett's office to check. But

174

whoever it had been, he'd left, and there was no sign of an attempted burglary, or anything like that. We didn't think to see if Uncle's gun was gone—who'd think of a thing like that? But that must have been what Laverne remembered."

Corrigan shook his head. "There's something missing, Mr. Craft, or it wasn't that at all. Even if that's what Miss Thomas had suddenly remembered, how would it have incriminated anyone if she didn't know who the visitor had been? Or," he said slowly, "did she?"

"I think she did," Craft said. "After we set the time vault that day, I recall Laverne's stooping to pick something up from the floor of Uncle Everett's office and saying, 'Oh, I know who this belongs to. I'll return it.' I was just going to ask her what it was she'd found, when the phone on my uncle's desk rang and I answered it. It was a customer, and we talked for some minutes. I think Laverne must have gone up the hall to return whatever it was, but she was back when I finally came out of Uncle Everett's office, and I didn't even ask her what it was all about. The phone call had made me completely forget the whole thing till just now."

"You didn't see the thing she picked up?"

Craft shook his head. "It had to have been something small, otherwise I'm sure I'd have spotted it, too, when we went into the office." His pale face looked worried as he glanced from Sally to Wanda to Turnboldt, and away. "I want to make clear that I don't know what the thing was or who it belonged to. Just in case somebody decides

I'm a—a danger to him—or her—too."

Wanda Hitchey looked daggers at him. Turnboldt seemed to be holding himself in check. Sally Peterson chuckled.

"Neatly put, Howie. In case it hasn't grabbed some of you yet, Howie's little speech ought to nail the point down that one of us is a homicidal maniac."

Wanda said, "A small object? You're always losing one of your earrings, Sally."

The blonde artist laughed. "Maybe it was a catnip leaf Laverne found, darling, and that would make it definitely you."

"That's enough," Corrigan said. "Anyone anything to add?"

No one did. So Corrigan told them to go back to sleep, and after they dispersed he took Maloney and Coats out into the hall. He told young Coats to return to Burns Accounting and the body of Brian Frank, and Maloney to shut himself up in Laverne Thomas's office.

"If I make an honest report on this case," Corrigan told them without heroics, "I'll find myself back on a beat. I should have had one of you guarding Frank's body from the start, and when the Thomas woman started babbling about trying to remember something I should have assigned the other one of you to guarding her. It's this end-of-the-world feeling; I can't account for my stupidity any other way. Let's not let this killer pull another smart one on us. We've got to guard whatever evidence there may be on the scenes of both murders for the lab boys. We're probably locking

176

the barn door, but maybe the horse is still there."

The two officers looked astounded at Corrigan's speech. But then they had never worked with him before.

Maloney returned with them to Burns Accounting to pick up his uniform overcoat; he hurried down the hall with a candle to Griswald Jewelers. Corrigan tried to phone headquarters again; the lines were still tied up, and this time he could not get the supervisor. He lit the candle on Sybil's desk and let Coats have his lantern back. Coats went into the accountants' room, leaving the door open; Corrigan waited until the lantern was out before he went over to the other office door and eased it open.

The room was dark, but by the light of the candle on the desk in the reception room he saw enough to tell him that she was back under the window bundled under the two coats.

He knelt beside her.

"I can kiss you with a clear conscience now," he said in a low voice. "Do you want us to take up where we left off?"

"Tim." She clung to him. But then she pushed. "Please don't misunderstand. But after this with Laverne—I mean, it would be ghoulish . . ."

"Sure, colleen, sure," he said gently; and kissed her, and rose, and shut the door behind him.

Corrigan took the candle from the desk and went into the accountants' room to get Brian Frank's topcoat from his locker. Young Coats rose quickly on one elbow, fumbling for his revolver. "It's just me, Coats," Corrigan said, gave him a noncommittal nod, and went out again.

He glanced at his watch before blowing out the candle.

It was twenty past midnight.

Unbelievable. He felt as if he had been prowling the twenty-first floor of the Bower Building for at least a year.

And as a bed the top of Sybil's desk compared unfavorably with Plymouth Rock.

Sybil's arms, he thought, would have been a lot softer.

He fell asleep.

Corrigan awoke from oblivion with a blazing light in his eyes. He sat up abruptly. The ceiling fixture was lit up; so was Sybil's desk lamp.

He looked at his watch, 5:28.

A.M., because there was the faintest daylight in the hall. The wall clock still registered 5:18, but the red second hand was moving. The power had just gone on.

It wasn't going to be a great deal of trouble for people throughout the city to reset their clocks, he thought. The electricity had been out for exactly twelve hours and ten minutes.

The ceiling light was burning in the accountants' room, too. Officer Coats came to the door and blinked at Corrigan.

"Morning, sir. Looks like we're back to normal."

"That," Corrigan said grimly, "is going to take a little time."

Coats disappeared again, presumably to find his shoes. Corrigan put on his, rubbed the sleep out of his eyes, and phoned the Detective Bureau. By a miracle the call went through. Lieutenant Ed Tagger was commanding the swing trick. Corrigan briefed him on the situation and requested a radio car team to relieve Coats and Maloney, a lab and a fingerprint team, a medic, a photographer, and a morgue wagon.

"I'll also need a stenographer," Corrigan said. "It'll be simpler to take statements here than to drag everybody down to headquarters. But I won't need the steno till later—say around ten. Soon as I put the tech boys to work, I want to run home to shower and shave."

"Will do," Tagger said. "I'll have replacements for the two officers there in ten minutes. The others as soon as I can."

As Corrigan hung up, Jeff Ring looked in. His eyes were red-rimmed and he was carrying his head like a basket of eggs.

"Everybody's up, Captain," Ring said. "Are we allowed to go home?"

"I'll be over to talk to you all in a minute," Corrigan said.

Coats had come out of the other room. "Mind if I go to the can, Captain?"

Corrigan nodded, and the man went out. Corrigan looked into the room where Sybil was parked. She was still cuddled under the two coats.

He turned on the ceiling light. Sybil started, blinked, and sat up. He surveyed her with approval. She was as attractive mussed as without

179

a hair out of place.

"The power's back on!" She yawned. "What time is it?"

"Little after five-thirty."

She made a face. "It's almost too late to go home, but I guess I will anyway."

"You must have the capacity of a lady camel," Corrigan grinned. "I don't recall your going to the john last night. Better do it."

"Aren't you fresh!" She jumped up and slipped on her shoes. "You see everything, don't you? It would be awfully hard for a girl to live with you."

"Maybe not," he said, and took a step.

"Now *now*," Sybil said, gave him her most Irish smile, grabbed her purse, and made for the ladies' room.

"Come over to the Adams' office when you're through," he called after her.

He decided he could use some of the lavatory's facilities himself. He went to the men's room.

By the time the occupants of the twenty-first floor had finished their toilettes, the relief team for Coats and Maloney had shown up. One was an overweight veteran, Sergeant Benz, his partner a rookie named Wheeler. Corrigan stationed Wheeler at the elevator to steer arriving police personnel to him and to keep the doors to Griswald Jewelers and Burns Accounting under observation so that no one without authorization might blunder into the murder rooms. Sergeant Benz he kept with him.

Eva Benson had made instant coffee by the time they all gathered in the main office of the Adams

180

Advertising Agency. Ring and Turnboldt were first with their cups; both seemed to have bad hangovers. Sally Peterson looked peaked; the others were in surprisingly good shape.

At Corrigan's appearance there was a clamor for permission to go home. Corrigan told them that a police stenographer was scheduled to arrive at 10 A.M. to take down their formal statements; if they could arrange to be back by then, they might leave at once.

"I planned to phone in sick," Wanda Hitchey objected. "I didn't sleep a wink on that damned ladies' room divan."

"It's here or police headquarters," Corrigan told her curtly. "Your choice."

Everyone decided to come back.

"Even with the power back on, you may run into a transportation problem. The subways won't be running normally for hours yet. So give yourselves some leeway."

"How do you figure that?" Turnboldt growled.

"Early last night the radio reported over six hundred trains stalled in tunnels, with something like eight hundred thousand passengers. I imagine they'll unload those who couldn't get out without picking up any new passengers; then they'll have to put on fresh crews before they resume their regular runs. I live at the Brookfield. If anybody's headed in that direction, I'll be glad to drop you off."

Sybil Graves said in a tone of profound astonishment, "I live at the Thaxton Apartments."

The Thaxton Apartments were no more than a hundred yards from the Brookfield.

Which pointed up one of the foul-ups of a big city, Corrigan thought. He would probably have met Sybil years ago if they had lived in Podunk.

No one else availed himself of Corrigan's offer. Ring and Turnboldt, who lived on Long Island, decided not to attempt the trip and settled on a Turkish bath and a barber shop in town. Howie Craft, who resided in Brooklyn, decided after some nail-worrying to accompany them. Sally Peterson, Mrs. Benson, and Wanda Hitchey all lived in Manhattan, Sally and Wanda within easy bus range. Eva had phoned her young husband and he was coming to pick her up in their car. He had spent the night, it seemed, having nightmares about her predicament; indeed, when Corrigan walked in, she was still on the phone, and several others were yapping at her for monopolizing it.

They had all taken off but Corrigan and Sybil by the time the technicians began to arrive, about 6 A.M. A young M.E. was first. He examined both bodies; but since the times of death were known, he had little to contribute. He told Corrigan he would be sent copies of the autopsy reports and scuttled off before the others got there.

The laboratory men and the stenographer showed up in his wake. The lab team consisted of a general technician named Mauthe and a finger-print expert, Powers. The civilian photographer Corrigan had worked with before, a man named Ball.

Corrigan took them first to the room where

Brian Frank's body still lay, and explained in detail what he wanted. He was especially interested, he told Ball, in some good closeups of the murder weapon, showing the safety on, before anyone touched it. Then he led the trio to Laverne Thomas's body and told them what he wanted done there.

"I'll be gone maybe three hours," he concluded. "You don't have to wait around. Anything you feel I ought to get right away leave with Sergeant Benz. Otherwise just put it in your reports."

He had some instructions for Officers Benz and Wheeler, too. "Everybody official, who's due, except for the morgue personnel, has now arrived. Soon as they're finished and give you the word, release the bodies for removal. Here's the M.E.'s order."

"Yes, sir," Benz said. "That'll leave us all alone here until people start coming to work. Want us to stick around?"

Corrigan nodded. "I'll be back at nine." By his watch it was twenty-five past six. He said to Sybil, "Let's get going, Irish. I need that shower."

19.

It was seven o'clock when he dropped Sybil off at her building. He gave her an hour to shower and dress, picked her up again at eight, and took her to breakfast.

From the restaurant he phoned the Main Office Squad to report to Inspector Macelyn what he was working on and where he would be. He and Sybil got back to the Bower Building at a few minutes to nine.

Mauthe, Powers, and Ball were long gone. Powers had left word with Sergeant Benz that there were no fingerprints on either murder weapon. Nothing of importance had been found.

The morgue wagon had also been there; the bodies were gone.

Benz reported that a couple of workers had arrived at the Adams Ad Agency, but so far no one had appeared at either Burns Accounting or Griswald Jewelers.

The sergeant, his rookie partner, Corrigan, and

Sybil were standing in the hall at the elevator as Benz made his report. Just as he concluded, the elevator opened and a thickset balding man with a red face, about forty, stepped out of the car.

The man greeted Sybil cordially; he looked curiously at the two uniformed men and Corrigan. He seemed fascinated by Corrigan's eye patch; he kept going back to it when he thought Corrigan wasn't looking.

Sybil introduced him as Gil Stoner; her voice was strained, and it made Stoner forget Corrigan's patch.

"What's wrong, Sybil? Why the cops? Griswald's been robbed again?" He had a beery sort of voice; thick and gurgly.

Corrigan put his hand on Stoner's arm. "You'd better come with me, Mr. Stoner."

"I don't get it," the accountant complained. "Does it have something to do with the blackout? Were you stuck here all night?"

Corrigan said abruptly. "Brian Frank and Laverne Thomas were murdered last night."

The man turned to stone. Corrigan was watching him closely. He saw the blood drain out of Stoner's face. "Mmmurdered? Brian? Laverne? Here? You're joking!"

"It's no joke, Mr. Stoner. Let's go over to your office and talk about it."

"Yes," the accountant said. "Of course." His eyes were glazed.

Corrigan left the two officers at the elevator. He took Stoner's arm firmly and half hustled him up the corridor to 2101. Sybil pattering along behind them.

Stoner stopped in the doorway. There was nothing to be seen in the reception room, but he kept looking around. He seemed to be avoiding the closed door to the accountants' office.

Corrigan said, "It happened in there," and gave Stoner the slightest push. The man actually staggered. Corrigan had to lead him to the door.

The body was gone, but no one had cleaned the office. Stoner turned green at the sight of the blood, the bits of flesh and brain matter spattered on Brian Frank's desk. He backed out into the reception room, gagging.

"If it's all the same to you, Captain, I'd rather not talk in—in there."

"Hard to stomach, eh, Mr. Stoner?"

"It's ghastly! Who'd do a thing like that?"

"It's done all the time," Corrigan said dryly, "and by the nicest people. Would you be more comfortable in the boss's office?"

"*Please.*"

Corrigan was puzzled. With Sybil eliminated, Stoner was his hottest suspect. Yet the man's reaction had seemed genuine. The way he had turned white, then green, the glaze in his eyes— these were physical symptoms of shock and nausea that were difficult, if not impossible, to simulate. If Stoner had pulled the two homicides he had lost a career on the stage. Corrigan did not believe in miracles. He was beginning to feel very dispirited.

In Carleton Burns's office Stoner took off his coat and hat and looked around uncertainly. Finally he dropped them on the floor. Corrigan picked them up and placed them on an end table. Stoner sank into one of the chairs. Sybil lingered in the doorway with a sick look on her face.

"Just what happened, Captain?" the accountant muttered.

"I'll explain it all in good time," Corrigan said. "First, Mr. Stoner, tell me where you spent last night."

Stoner looked up. "Me? I don't understand. Don't you know who killed Brian and Laverne?"

"Please answer my question."

The glaze disappeared. The man seemed to draw himself in. "I see. By asking where I spent last night, you're implying that I'm under suspicion?"

"At the moment, Mr. Stoner, everyone who had motive and opportunity is under suspicion."

"Motive?"

"It seems to be common knowledge on this floor that Brian Frank and your wife were having an affair. You had a violent scene with him about it."

Gil Stoner blinked. After a long time he said slowly, "What time do I have to cover to prove I didn't have opportunity?"

"You left the office at four-thirty, according to my information. You can take it from there."

The accountant said very carefully, "I went straight from the office to Luke's Tavern over on Eleventh. I stop there every night on my way home. I had a couple of beers with a friend named Harry Blake. Harry works around here and lives in the same building I do in Brooklyn. We left Luke's—together—a few minutes past five and caught a BMT train. On the way to Brooklyn the power conked out. We spent the rest of the night in a tunnel on the train."

"You were with this Harry Blake all night, then?"

"From about twenty to five, when we met at Luke's, till we got off the train around twenty to six this morning."

So it wasn't Stoner. But he had to check it out.

"How do I get in touch with Blake?"

"He works for the Bonn Brokerage Company up the street. B-o-n-n. I know he's there now, because we ride in to work together, too."

A stack of telephone directories lay on a small table near Burns's desk. Corrigan looked up the number of the brokerage firm in the Manhattan book. He asked for Harry Blake. Harry Blake confirmed Stoner's story.

Corrigan had just hung up when a spare, rather handsome white-haired old man wearing a black homburg appeared beside Sybil in the doorway and looked keenly from Corrigan to Stoner.

Sybil said nervously, "This is Captain Corrigan of the police, Mr. Burns."

Carleton Burns came into the room. He looked at the ashen-faced accountant, he looked at Corrigan's patch.

"What's going on here?" He had a soft, old-man's voice, just the least bit quavery.

Corrigan said, "You don't know about the murders, Mr. Burns?"

The white-haired man stopped in the act of removing his topcoat. But it was just for a moment. Then he completed the operation, hung the coat and his hat precisely on a clothes tree. He glanced at Sybil, still standing in the doorway, and went over and deliberately shut the door in her face. He came back and sat down behind his desk. He looked around, rose, retrieved the cushion from the floor near the window, placed it on the chair, and sat down again.

Only then did he say, "Murders? What murders, sir?"

Corrigan gave him a resume of the night's events. Stoner, forgotten for the moment, listened to the details as intently as the old man did. If Carleton Burns was shocked by the news, he did not show it. Tough old bird, Corrigan thought.

"I'm sorry, Captain. I liked Miss Thomas. It's all hard to believe." He paused. "I didn't know Frank very well—he'd only been with us four months or so. But I've known Miss Thomas for years."

Corrigan said, "How did you spend last night, Mr. Burns?"

If the old man realized that he was being asked to produce an alibi, he failed to show it.

"Luckily I hadn't boarded a train when the power went off," old Burns said. "I was waiting on the platform. When we all realized that the electricity wasn't going to come back on right away, people climbed back to the street, I among them. It was quite a night—matches and lighters being held aloft wherever you looked. I made my way to the lobby of the old Queen Anne Hotel up the street, sat there for about an hour, and finally decided the blackout was going to last indefinitely.

189

I tried to phone home, couldn't get an open line, and checked into the hotel. I had dinner in my room by candlelight. Quite romantic if you're twenty-five, I suppose. I'm sixty-seven and it depressed me."

"You were alone the whole time, Mr. Burns?"

"I'm afraid I was, Captain," Carleton Burns said imperturbably.

No alibi. But Burns had no known motive for Frank's murder. Unless one emerged, Corrigan saw no reason to list the head of Burns Accounting as more than the remotest suspect.

"Does either of you gentlemen have any idea who might have wanted Brian Frank dead?"

The white head shook emphatically. "I really know nothing about the man aside from his work record, Captain. He was a competent accountant, and that's all I cared about."

Stoner said suddenly, "I know about a threat he'd had, but it wasn't a death threat. At least Brian didn't consider it one. He only expected a beating."

Corrigan barked, "Let's have it!"

"Well, up to the other day Brian and I were pretty friendly. He used to tell me a lot about his personal affairs."

Except the one with Mrs. Stoner, Corrigan thought.

"Like what?"

"Well, his horse-playing, mostly."

"Frank played the horses?" Carleton Burns exclaimed. His face had darkened. "If I'd known that, he'd have been fired on the spot! A reputable

190

accountancy firm—''

"Please, Mr. Burns," Corrigan said. "What about Frank's horse-playing, Mr. Stoner?"

"He told me he had a marker in for twenty-five hundred dollars with a bookmaker named Potts."

"Track-Odds Potts?"

"Yes. Yes, that's the one. I remember Brian mentioning it. He was all upset because this Potts had given him an ultimatum to pay up. 'Or else' kind of stuff. He said if he couldn't come up with the money by a certain date—he didn't tell me when—a couple of Potts' strong-arm boys would catch him alone one day and beat him up. I actually asked him if there was danger of Potts having him killed. He didn't seem worried about that. He said bookies don't kill welshers, because they can't collect from a dead man."

It was not necessarily so. Bookies sometimes ordered welshers hit as object lessons to other delinquents. Corrigan knew Herman (Track-Odds) Potts too well, however, to credit him with a fancy hit like this. Potts's speed was to have a pair of his musclemen catch the victim in an alley, where one would hold him while the other beat him over the head with a section of rubber hose; in chronic cases, a lead pipe.

On the other hand, any detective on a murder case in which the victim had been threatened by a bookie would deserve to lose his shield if he failed to check it out. He made a mental note.

The door burst open. Corrigan knew who it was before he turned around. Chuck Baer never knocked.

"Oh, excuse me," Baer said, but instead of backing out he came in. "MOS said you were still here, Tim."

"And a better morning to you than it's been to me," Corrigan said. He introduced the private detective, who promptly beckoned Corrigan to a far corner of the room, lit up one of his endless supply of panetelas, and grunted, "I stopped by to give you a tip. Know Joseph Mattucci?"

"Just enough to nod to. He'll never be the private eye you are. What about him?"

"Joe and I are working an insurance case together; we had breakfast this morning to talk business. I mentioned last night, and it turns out Joe knew Brian Frank."

"Oh?" Corrigan said. "What's the scoop?"

"Seems Frank was the villain of the piece in a case Joe investigated six months or so ago."

"What kind of case?"

"Blackmail."

Corrigan hiked the brow over his eye. "Frank was the blackmailer?"

"You've got a high IQ, Captain. That he was. Joe's client was a married chick Frank was putting the squeeze on. He threatened to expose their affair to her hubby unless she paid off."

"What happened?"

"Joe scared the peewaddin' out of him. Frank decided he'd tackled the wrong pigeon and took off."

Corrigan thought for a moment. Until now he had been visualizing Brian Frank as a run-of-the-mill office-type lecher, but otherwise good at his job and no worse than the next man. Baer's information put the dead accountant in a depressing light. On top of his horse-betting and debts, he had not been above philandering for extortion purposes. He began to shape up as an all-round nogoodnik.

Corrigan made a sudden decision. "Tell that story to Mr. Burns and Mr. Stoner," he said to Chuck Baer.

Baer looked surprised. But he rarely questioned Corrigan's decisions. He shrugged. They went back to where the two men were waiting, and he told them what he had told Corrigan.

20.

Corrigan studied Gil Stoner while Baer made his spiel. The accountant turned a faded red. But since Carleton Burns apparently had no knowledge of the relationship between Brian Frank and Stoner's wife, Corrigan tabled the obvious questions until he could get the accountant alone.

Old Mr. Burns shook his head. "And I thought I could judge character. First I learn the man was a chronic gambler, now that he was also a seducer and a blackmailer. It's certainly going to affect my firm's image if all this is made public." Burns looked at Baer. "Did I understand Captain Corrigan to say you're a private detective, Mr. Baer?"

"That's right."

The old man shifted to Corrigan. "Can you recommend this man, Captain?"

Corrigan smiled. "I hate to do it in front of him, Mr. Burns, but truth compels me to recommend him unconditionally."

"I think I had best take some preventive measures, Mr. Baer. We have some highly conservative clients who'd frown on doing business with an accounting firm that employed a man like Brian Frank. First, I'd like to engage you to make a thorough investigation of Mr. Frank's background to see if there's anything else in his background that might reflect on my company."

"That's first," Baer nodded. "what's second, Mr. Burns?"

"I want you to make every effort to keep the details of Mr. Frank's vices out of the news media."

Not once as the old man spoke did he look at Corrigan. Corrigan had to stifle a grin. The old fox! He'd spotted the Corrigan-Baer buddyship instantly, and he was deliberately putting the pressure on the police officer in charge to withhold from the newsmen Frank's unsavory background in the interest of helping old buddy out. Old Burns must know that the likeliest source of information to the press was the police, and without Corrigan's cooperation Baer hadn't a chance.

The big redhead said gravely, "No guarantees on number two, Mr. Burns. Do my best, okay. But I don't warrant my best will be good enough."

"Just do your best, Mr. Baer," the old shrewdie said.

"Then it's a deal, Mr. Burns. My standard fee is a hundred a day plus expenses." Corrigan had to turn away. Chuck's standard fee was seventy-five a day plus expenses; old buddy was paying his new client back in kind.

The old man waved, "Bill me personally, of course. I'd rather not have the expense appear on the books of the Burns Accounting Company."

Sergeant Benz stuck his head in the door. "Excuse me, Captain, but there's a bunch of reporters here. What do I tell them?"

"I'll see them," Corrigan said. "Mr. Stoner, I'd like to see you privately after I finish out there, so please stick around."

Baer trailed along. Corrigan gave the newsmen waiting in the hall a capsule briefing on the two murders, then adroitly fielded their questions. He found himself neglecting to mention that Brian Frank had been a womanizer, a welshing horse better, and an extortionist.

"You bum," he said to Baer when the newsmen were herded off the twenty-first floor. "Look at the spot you put me in. They'll crucify me when they find out."

"Talking about spots," Baer said indignantly, "you're a hell of a pal. Any more bombshells like Laverne Thomas's knockoff after I left last night?"

"I never got a chance to tell you." He briefed Baer on the events of the night after Baer's departure.

"You haven't exactly covered yourself with glory on this case," Baer said when Corrigan concluded. "I'm surprised at you."

"That's right, rub it in!"

"That little piece of Irish fluff couldn't have anything to do with your goof-off, could she?"

"I don't know what you're talking about," Corrigan said angrily; and he stuck his head into

Carleton Burns's office and gruffly beckoned Gil Stoner out.

"I take it, Stoner, your boss Mr. Burns in there doesn't know anything about the trouble you had with Frank."

"No," Stoner said, flushing. "I appreciate your not bringing it up in front of him, Captain. He's like Queen Victoria about scandal in the office. He'd fire me sure if he found out about my wife."

Corrigan barked, "Was Frank blackmailing Mrs. Stoner?"

The balding accountant glanced uneasily at Chuck Baer. "Does Mr. Baer have to be in on this?"

"He's not going to repeat anything," Corrigan said grimly. "How about answering my question?"

"Lois didn't mention blackmail. Though it's true we haven't been having much conversation lately."

"How'd you find out about Frank and your wife?"

"I got an anonymous letter in last Saturday's mail."

"Do you still have it?"

Stoner shook his head. "After I had it out with Lois I tore it up."

Another idiot. Corrigan grumbled to himself. He couldn't count the times investigations had been made more difficult for him because such vital clues as extortion notes or ransom notes had been burned or flushed down a toilet.

"What kind of note was it? And what did it say?"

"It was typed. No date, no return address. I

197

remember the damn thing word for word. 'Wake up, sucker. Ask your wife where she goes on your lodge and bowling nights. Show her photo to the night desk clerk at the Kaxton Hotel. He'll tell you that on those nights she's been checking into a double room with a Mr. James Smith as Mrs. Smith.' It was signed, 'A Friend.'"

Baer said, "Friends like that a guy doesn't need."

Corrigan said to the accountant, "On receipt of the letter, you confronted your wife with it?"

"Not right off; she was away shopping. I drove down to the Kaxton with a snapshot of her. The night clerk was off duty, but he lived there and I booted him out of bed. Ten bucks got him talking. Lois had been checking in there with a guy on nights when I was out, all right. His description fitted Brian, but I couldn't believe it."

"Why?"

"He was supposed to be a friend of mine."

And you're a first-class jerk, Corrigan told him silently. It was the "friends" who made the scene with the little woman nine times out of ten. Aloud he said, "Did you make a positive identification, Stoner? Find out definitely that Brian Frank was the man?"

"I sure did. When Lois got home I tossed the letter at her and told her what the Kaxton's night clerk had said. We went round and round, but finally she admitted it was Brian. She practically spat his name at me, as though she hoped I'd beat hell out of him, too."

Corrigan didn't miss the "too." "She was sore at him, then?"

"She's sore at the world. But at me mainly. His name was practically the last thing she's said to me. Since then she's clammed up—gives me the freeze."

Baer said suddenly, "What's your address, Stoner?"

The man looked startled. "Why?"

"I want to talk to your wife, to find out if Frank was blackmailing her. Or would you rather I get your address from Mr. Burns?"

His boss's name was the magic word. Stoner gave Baer a Brooklyn address, in the Prospect Park area.

"That's all, Stoner," Corrigan said. "You can go back to work."

"If you think I'm putting a foot in that bloody office, you're out of your mind! Unless Mr. Burns has some outside assignment for me, I'm taking the day off."

"In that case," Baer said, "I'll drive you home."

"Who the hell wants to go home?" Stoner cried. "I'm spending the day in a bar."

He shambled back into 2101.

"Poor devil," Corrigan said. "If I had a wife who gave out for my friends, I wouldn't have made it past the first tavern I saw on my way to work."

"If she was my wife, she wouldn't have made it past the first tavern I saw on my way to work."

"If she was my wife, she wouldn't be giving out for anyone else," Baer retorted.

"Sometimes I can hardly stand you! Go talk to the dame and let me know how you make out. It'll save me a trip to Brooklyn. That desk was hard last night."

When Baer left, Corrigan hooked his index finger at Sergeant Benz, and the overweight policeman waddled over. "Anyone show at Griswald's yet?"

"Mr. Griswald, Captain. He asked me and Wheeler what we were doing here and we told him about the murders. Was that all right?"

Corrigan shrugged. "They're no secret."

He went down the hall to 2102 and walked into the display room. It was empty. Through the open door to his left he could see an old man seated behind the desk. He was tiny; he could not have weighed more than a hundred and twenty pounds. He had a shiny head without a hair and the skin of an elephant, hard-wrinkled and gray. Bright, predatory eyes peered over gold-rimmed glasses that rested on the end of a big nose. Corrigan put his age at seventy-five, maybe older.

"Mr. Griswald?"

"Yes?" The voice was cracked and waspish.

"I'm Captain Corrigan of the Main Office Squad, in charge of the investigation here."

Old Griswald waved the piece of scratch paper in his hand. "Do you know about this? Did you talk to that thumbsucker? I mean my nephew?"

Corrigan walked over for the paper:

Dear Uncle Everett:

I was stuck here all night. By the time you see this, I imagine you will have heard about Brian Frank and poor Laverne. I've gone out for a steam bath, a shave, and breakfast.

Sorry, but I'll be back at 10:00, or as close to it as I can.

Howard

Corrigan handed the note back. "What's the point, Mr. Griswald?"

"We open at nine, not ten," Griswald rasped. He waved a claw at the wall clock, which Corrigan noted had been reset to the correct time. "It's already past nine-thirty, and the jewelry isn't even on display!"

In his trade Corrigan met all kinds of characters, but Everett Griswald was new even for him. His one eye looked the old Scrooge over with curiosity.

"What's the matter with you?" asked Griswald querulously. "What are you looking at me that way for?"

"Is opening for business all you can think about this morning, Mr. Griswald?"

The old man stared at him. "It's my place of business. It's got to open on time." He sounded positively nonplused, as if Corrigan had asked him if two and two didn't make five.

"Last night a woman who'd worked for you for twenty years or more was murdered in cold blood not forty feet from where you're sitting. Doesn't that mean anything to you?"

"Sure. I'm very sorry."

"You don't sound it."

"Look here, Mr. Officer! I don't like your tone of voice! Will not opening for business bring Laverne back to life? I'm a businessman. Business is business!"

Corrigan shrugged. It was useless. "Have you tried your safe yet?"

The feeling old Griswald might have been expected to display over the death of Laverne Thomas leaped into his watery eyes at Corrigan's question. "What do you mean? What do you mean have I tried the safe yet? Is something—did somebody—" He jumped out of his chair like a cricket.

"It's electric," Corrigan said, watching him as he would a specimen. "The lock didn't release at nine A.M. because the power was off for twelve hours and ten minutes. It won't open till ten after nine tonight, Mr. Griswald. So sometimes business is shot to hell, right?"

The old man sat down, looking relieved. But as he thought Corrigan's facts over, his gray face darkened.

"A whole day wasted!"

"Maybe you can sell tickets to the scene of the crime," Corrigan said. "That's a joke, dad. I'll be using Miss Thomas's office to take formal statements from witnesses, so don't plan on using it for anything else for a while." Corrigan turned on his heel and stalked out.

Another uniformed man was waiting in the hall with Benz and Wheeler. He was the stenographer from headquarters.

21.

According to the name cards under the mailboxes in the lobby, the Stoner apartment was on the third floor. Chuck Baer pushed the bell button, and right away the lock on the door buzzed.

The private detective climbed the stairs. A woman waited in the doorway of an apartment on the third floor, looking hopeful.

That kind, Baer thought. Anything in pants. She wasn't worrying about rape.

He examined her critically as he closed the distance between them. She was a bottle-blonde, about thirty, with a curvy figure beginning to run to fat. She was wearing bedroom slippers and a print housedress without a brassiere. Her face would have been pretty in a petulant way except for the puffy slit of a shiner on her right eye. It was several days old; it had turned purplish yellow.

The woman had been looking Baer over just as thoroughly. The breadth of his shoulders was already kindling her undamaged eye.

Baer took off his hat. "Mrs. Stoner?"

"I'm Lois Stoner. Who are you and what do you want?" The words said one thing, the tone something entirely different. Long ago she had developed the tiny simpery voice of the patented sexpot.

"My name is Chuck Baer. I'm a private detective."

That was different. "Yeah?" The fire was quenched; the tone became back-alley. It said, What's your angle? Aloud she said, "So what?"

"May I come in?"

She did not move. "Depends on what you want, mister. Some subjects I got a tight lip."

Baer smiled. "I haven't been hired by your husband, Mrs. Stoner, if that's what you're worried about."

"Why would that worry me?" But it seemed to him she relaxed slightly.

"Brian Frank."

She eyed him. "I don't know what you're talking about. If you'll be so good as to excuse me—"

Baer said patiently, "I'm not making a divorce investigation, so I don't give a damn if you've got a lover in every hotel in town. Frank was shot to death last night."

Her unpuffed eye went wide. "Brian dead? Was it—did Gil—"

"The police don't know who murdered him, but I believe your husband has an alibi. We don't want to entertain the neighbors, do we, Mrs. Stoner? How about inviting me in?"

She stepped back jerkily. Baer brushed past her into a cramped, cheaply furnished front room. He shoved the door shut with a reverse kick, and she fell back against it.

"How come a private eye is working on a murder?" she asked. "What's your interest in it?"

"Frank's boss hired me to look into it." He looked around.

"Oh, Mr. Burns." She straightened up from the door and waved toward a sofa. "Just drop your hat and coat there. What did you say your name was?"

She got over the shock of lover-boy's death pretty quick, Baer thought. One of those till-death-do-us-part quickies.

"Chuck Baer."

"Glad to know you, Chuck." The little sexpot voice was back. Quickie was right. "I'm the informal type, Chuck. You can call me Lois, or Lo. Sweet and Lo, that's me." She chuckled.

Baer tossed his coat and hat on the sofa and dropped beside them. "And hot, I take it."

"Boiling, Chuck." She had gone over to an upholstered chair facing the sofa and perched on one arm, one buttock and leg dangling. The dangling leg began to swing a little, hiking the short dress up. She had nothing on underneath below the waist, either.

"Nice view," Baer said companionably, and lit a panetela, surveying the scene.

"What? Oh!" she said, and slid down into the chair. "You will have to forgive me, Chuck. I wasn't expecting anybody."

"It's okay with me," Baer said. He puffed,

looked around for an ashtray, pulled one over to him, and said, "Who gave you that shiner, Lois? Frank or Gil?"

Her face darkened with rage. "The lousy wife-beater!"

"Just wanted to confirm the story," he nodded. "Well, you have to admit you gave Gil a reason."

"What do you know about it?" she asked sullenly.

"About you and Brian Frank? All there *is*. The anonymous letter hubby got. His trip to the Kaxton. How he slammed you around till you admitted Frank was your lover."

"You think you know so much! If Gil had stopped to listen, he wouldn't have blown so high. The thing with Brian was all over by the time that damn letter came. I hated Brian's guts. You don't see me shedding any tears at the news that he's dead, do you?"

"I figured you're the hit-and-run type. What's your beef against the dead man?"

"He was a lousy blackmailer. And a dumb one at that. You know who mailed that letter to Gil?"

"Who?"

"Brian mailed it himself! The idea was that I'd open it, it would scare my pants off, and I'd pay up and not show it to Gil. Only the stupid jerk mailed it so it came Saturday morning, when Gil was home. Brian never meant Gil to see it."

This clarified a point that had been puzzling Baer ever since he had heard of the letter. Once Gil Stoner received it, all chance of collecting blackmail was blown. Baer had never even considered the possibility that the blackmailer himself had sent it. Jerk was right. If it was true.

"Do you know this to be a fact, Lois, or are you guessing what happened?"

"I phoned the s.o.b. at his apartment right after Gil gave me the shiner and took off. Brian said yes, he'd sent the letter. He was more upset than I was that Gil received it instead of me. He kept saying he'd only mailed it that morning, and it shouldn't have got here till Monday." Her smeary lips curved in vindictively. "Score one for the post office."

"Was that the whole conversation?"

"Hell, no. He wanted to know if I'd told Gil he was the man involved. I said, 'Sure I did, you bum, and he's on his way over there right now to kill you.' Then I hung up on him. You say it wasn't Gil who killed him?"

Baer said, "You sound as though you wish he had."

She shrugged. "I should care if Gil takes a bust for murder? There isn't a thing left between us. Do you think I'd have gone into the hay with Brian Frank if there had been?"

"You want an honest answer, Lois?" Baer said. "Yes."

She snarled at him. "Well, for your information, Mr. Detective, I wasn't always this way. Gil thinks any girl who wants it more than once a month is oversexed. I've got a warm nature. Brian wasn't the first guy since I married Gil, and he won't be the last. I need a man on a regular basis." She leaned back in open invitation. "Now like you, for instance. You look like you could make a girl happy, if you gather my meaning."

The question was, Baer speculated, not how many men she had slept with, but whether Frank was the first one her husband had found out about. As for her invitation of the moment, he was not a dilettante of the bedroom, but he drew the line at tarts. She probably offered herself to every salesman, meter inspector, and teenage delivery boy who came to her door.

He decided to cool it in the bud.

"I'd like to oblige you, baby, but your husband took the day off. He could walk in any minute. I'd hate to be responsible for you getting your other eye shined up."

She jumped as if he had thrown a spitball at her. "Gil's coming home?"

Baer got to his feet. "I think I'd better blow."

She insisted on holding his coat for him. At the door she stood unnecessarily close.

"You could stop by tomorrow morning," she said coyly.

"I'll see what my schedule is. By the way. How did you get together with Brian Frank originally?"

"What?" She had apparently forgotten her dead lover altogether. "Oh, how did we get chummy? Gil brought him home to dinner one night."

"How well did you get to know Frank?"

She giggled. "How much better can a woman know a man?"

"I mean, did you know much about him outside his bedroom stunts? For instance, any trouble he'd ever been in?"

She shook her head. "I never heard of him until about two and a half months ago."

He nodded, walked around her, and opened the door.

"How about tomorrow, Chuck?" she asked eagerly. "Shall I expect you?"

"Not unless I phone first." He stepped quickly out into the hall before she could throw her arms around his neck.

She looked neither offended nor disappointed. She stood in the doorway watching him until he disappeared around the next landing.

She hadn't even asked how her lover died, Baer thought. Now there was a one-track mind.

22.

All the witnesses were back on the twenty-first floor by 10 A.M. By noon, Corrigan had formal statements from the lot.

He took Sybil to lunch in a Chinese joint, and over the chow mein learned that she did not have to return to the office. Carleton Burns had told her she could take the afternoon off.

"He's kind of a nice old guy," Sybil said. "He didn't have to let me off, because he's working all afternoon himself and probably could have used me. But he knew I was upset about Brian. Old Mr. Griswald gave Howard Craft the afternoon off, too, but not for the same reason."

"The safe?" Corrigan grinned.

Sybil nodded. "They can't get their stock out of it. He'll dock Howie for the time off."

"His own nephew?"

"That old miser would dock his mother."

Corrigan dropped Sybil at her apartment. She looked into the car window to thank him, and he said, "Busy this evening?"

"No."

"How about having dinner with me?"

"I'd love it, Tim."

That was one of the things he liked about her. She didn't play games. The rules said she should have pleaded a previous date. She was as direct as he was.

He grinned at her and said he would pick her up at six-thirty.

He drove down to headquarters. Inspector Macelyn was just walking into the MOS squad-room from lunch. They went into Macelyn's office and Corrigan gave the inspector a report on his progress. Then he shut himself up in his own bare ten-by-twelve cubby, read his mail and the morning teletype, and then phoned the police lab and asked for Ray Yoder.

When the Chief Criminalist came on, Corrigan said, "Anything on the double murder at the Bower Building yet, Ray?"

"What do you want to know?"

"Anything."

"I'm afraid it's all negative, Tim. Presumably the bullet that killed Brian Frank came from the P38. The bullet in the baseboard was too banged-up for comparison, but it was the right caliber, and one shell had been fired from the pistol. It was a soft-nosed, flat-headed slug."

"What about the weapon in the Laverne Thomas kill?"

"What about it? I understand Powers left word for you that there were no fingerprints on either weapon."

"Yeah," Corrigan grunted. "Ray, I'm hunting for a handhold—anything. I have three strong possibles and a couple of remotes, but there I'm stuck."

"Sorry," Yoder said.

"Thanks!"

Corrigan left his office. At the Bureau of Criminal Identification he pulled the record of Herman (Track-Odds) Potts.

It was not the man's background he was interested in; he was familiar enough with that. All he wanted was Potts's current address. Like most bookies, Track-Odds had an unlisted telephone number.

As of his last arrest four months previously, the man was fixed in an apartment in the upper Eighties.

Corrigan went back to his office and phoned the Gambling Squad to find out if they knew whether he was still at that location.

"He was there a couple of weeks ago," Sergeant Morton said. "You know we make a periodic check on these jokers to keep track of them."

"In case he isn't home, where is Potts running his book now?"

Morton snorted. "That's a dumb question, Tim. If we knew, we'd shut him down."

"Any rumors?"

"The vine says he isn't running a parlor since his last bust. We think he's operating temporarily by phone from his own pad."

"Okay, Phil."

Corrigan hung up just as the door crashed in. It had to be Chuck Baer, and it was.

The private detective straddled the lone visitor's chair, unbuttoned his topcoat, and pushed his hat back. He leaned forward to knock ashes into Corrigan's ashtray from the panetela he was smoking.

"Make yourself at home," Corrigan growled.

"From your hospitable tone," Baer said gently, "you're getting nothing."

"You're so right. All I can figure is it's a tossup between Turnboldt, the Hitchey babe, and Sally Peterson. From the standpoint of opportunity."

"Don't go tagging Sally. We have a date tonight."

Corrigan relaxed. "Last night I got the impression that you struck out there."

"Not quite. She just called time out because that jerk Turnboldt walked in on us and cooled her off. I talked to her on the phone just a few minutes ago and she sounded crazy about me."

"What time's your date?"

"Early. I'm taking her to dinner."

"Ditto Sybil and me," Corrigan said. "How about making it a foursome?"

"As long as we split afterwards," the redhead grinned. "Whose car?"

"My date is for half-past six. I'll pick you up at six-fifteen."

"So much for the society page. Now how about business?"

"You saw Lois Stoner?"

"I sure did. You listening?"

213

"I'm two ears."

"First off, she's a nympho," Baer said. "Most of her conversation and actions added up to 'Let's hop into bed.'"

"Just like that?" Corrigan surveyed him. "You look fresh as a daisy."

"I passed," Baer said. "For all I know, I was the seventh guy to ring her bell today."

"I don't care how many broads you turn down," Corrigan said. "What's the scoop?"

"Brian Frank did try to blackmail her. And he sent Stoner that letter."

Corrigan looked surprised. "That's a hot one! Just her guess, or does she know?"

Baer related Lois Stoner's story. When he finished, Corrigan shook his head. "Now I've heard everything," he said. "Well, it's interesting, but I can't see that it gets us anywhere." He got up and put on his coat and hat.

"You going somewhere?" Baer asked without stirring.

"To have a little chin with Track-Odds Potts."

"Potts?" Baer shook his head. "How could the bookie be involved? I thought you'd reduced it to three suspects."

"Potts wouldn't hit anyone personally," Corrigan snapped. "He may have threatened one of the three into doing it—how do I know? One of them could owe him a bundle. Potts wouldn't be the first bookie to collect by forcing a welsher to exercise some muscle for him."

Baer considered this. Then he nodded and

214

climbed to his feet.

"I guess I'll tag along," he said.

It was an antiseptic apartment building of concrete, metal, and glass, as homey-looking as a warren. Some three hundred rabbits chewed their lettuce there.

Corrigan and Baer got off the elevator at the seventh floor and walked along a carpeted hall to a door numbered 727. There was a magnifying peepsight in the door. Corrigan stood in line with it and rang the bell.

After a while the door cracked open and a wide, flat, ape-like face peered out. Corrigan was familiar with it. It belonged to a longtime runner and muscleman who worked for Herman Potts. Its owner's name was Charles Stope, better known in professional circles as Charlie-the-Squeeze.

Corrigan gave the door a push. Charlie stepped back and let it open.

"You want something, Captain?" The man had a laryngitical voice.

"Potts."

Corrigan walked straight toward him, and Stope, who topped him by eight inches, stepped aside to avoid contact. When Chuck Baer started to follow, however, he balked.

"I don't know this guy. Who's he?"

"A friend of mine, Charlie," said Corrigan. "You know, any friend of mine is a friend of yours?"

Charlie-the-Squeeze looked unhappy, but he stopped blocking Baer's way. Baer looked disappointed.

"You guys got a warrant?" Charlie demanded.

"A search warrant is for searching," Corrigan explained in kindergarten tones. "We're not planning to search, Charlie. This is what you might term a social call. Long-time-no-see-Track-Odds. Kapish?"

"Uh," Charlie-the-Squeeze said. His two-inch brow looked like a plane's-eye view of an irrigation project. "Well, if you ain't gonna make no trouble," he said. He jerked his vast head. "He's in his bedroom getting a massodge."

"That's the boy," Corrigan said; and he strode across the ornate living room in the direction of the muscleman's headjerk, followed by Chuck Baer and Charlie-the-Squeeze in single file, and paused in the doorway for a preliminary look at what was going on inside.

Track-Odds Potts, all fat and a yard wide, lay naked on his squeezed stomach on a rubdown table, his rump covered with a towel. A muscular blond young giant, crew-cut and bare to the waist, was alternately kneading the rolls of fat on Potts' back and drumming on it with the edges of his hard hands. A wiry character in a black sharkskin suit was smoking a cigaret in a chair by the window. He looked dead.

The bookie's head swiveled on its fat neck. When he saw Corrigan his eyes hooded over like a snake's. Corrigan moved into the room. Baer came in, too; he took up a position against the wall, beside the door. Charlie-the-Squeeze stopped in the doorway, his head buried between his shoulders.

Corrigan said, "Afternoon, Herman." He looked at the man by the window. "Hi, Alfonze."

The bookie grunted hello; he sounded like a whale in pain. The face of the man by the window remained dead; only his nostrils showed a sign of life. Alfonze (Tip) Marks hated his baptismal name, which was why Corrigan used it.

The MOS man stopped at the foot of the rubdown table and looked from its gross occupant to the masseur. The barechested young man glanced, startled, at Corrigan's eye patch; then he returned his attention to his job. It seemed to Corrigan that the tempo of the tattoo increased.

It was the only sound in the room.

23.

Corrigan pointed a thumb at the young blond giant.

"Professional masseur, Herman, or a new boy on your payroll?"

Track-Odds Potts gave out a series of grunts in rhythm with the masseur's drumming before saying, "Hans? Yeah, he works for me."

Corrigan swung his eye to the dead-faced man by the window, then to Charlie-the-Squeeze. "You're carrying a lot of muscle for a guy who claims he's retired."

"Muscle?" Potts wheezed. "Tip is my social secretary. Charlie is my butler, and Hans is my trainer. What d'ye want?"

"To talk about Brian Frank."

"I pass," Potts said frantically.

"The guy who was plugged down at the Bower Building last night," Corrigan said. "I see you've heard about it."

"Is it a crime to listen to the radio? They said

there were two murders. Some old babe of a bookkeeper. You want to ask me about her, too, Captain?"

"I understand Frank was one of your customers."

"Customers?" Potts exclaimed. "I ain't even in business! Customer for what?"

"Look, Herman," Corrigan said. "I'm not interested in your bookie operation. I've got a couple of murders to worry about. Frank owed you twenty-five hundred dollars. That's what I want to talk about."

"I told you," Potts said. "I never heard of him."

Corrigan said patiently, "Don't give me a hard time, Herman. Do I have to squeeze it out of you?"

The blond masseur stopped drumming. He straightened up and hooked his thumbs in his belt. He seemed to be concentrating now on Corrigan's patch.

"Something on your mind, Hans?" Corrigan asked.

"The boss says he doesn't know the pigeon," Hans said. He had a high, almost feminine, voice. "Whatever the hell your name is."

"Captain Corrigan," Corrigan said, so quietly that the fat man on the rubbing table raised himself in alarm. "You may call me either Captain or Sir. Now what were we talking about, Herman?"

But Hans said, "You want the fuzz out, boss?"

Potts gave his small fat head an uneasy shake. It was one of those ambiguous movements whose interpretation depended on the interpreter.

Corrigan was sure that the bookie did not mean to give his new employee a go-ahead. The blond giant, however, chose to read it as a nod. Corrigan was unprepared; he had read Potts' headshake differently. Before he could set himself, the masseur had sprung, grabbed Corrigan's wrist, spun him around like a ballet partner, and held him immobilized in a hammerlock.

Chuck Baer moved forward by instinct. But for the moment he had forgotten about Charlie-the-Squeeze. Charlie-the-Squeeze, who was a bird of very little brain but lightning reflexes, reacted in character. He swung a looping chop with one of his ham hocks that caught Baer flush behind the ear.

The dead man in the chair had jumped to his feet. Fat Herman sat all the way up on the rubbing table and cried. "Hey! Hey! Hold it!"

He was too late.

Corrigan stomped on Hans's naked instep at the same instant that Baer spun around to look reproachfully at his vast attacker. Charlie was slowed up by amazement; he could not seem to understand why the redhead hadn't dropped in his tracks.

Charlie started to swing a left.

Hans had barely been able to get a squeal of pain out when Corrigan's heel smashed back against his kneecap, kicking his leg out from under him. He crumpled onto the injured knee, his grip on Corrigan's arm coming loose. Corrigan whirled to face him just as Baer blocked Charlie-the-Squeeze's left and countered with a hook that left a blur in its wake.

There was a splattering noise as Baer's fist connected. Corrigan had no time to appreciate its beauty. By then he had his back to Baer and Charlie-the-Squeeze. Hans was getting to his feet. Corrigan helped him all the way up by a *savate* that landed on his jaw. The kick actually brought young Hans to his tippy-toes. Then he toppled over on his back and lay still.

From the corner of his eye, Corrigan caught a glimpse of Tip Marks rushing him. He ducked under a right and hurled himself at the man's knees. Mark's legs came to an abrupt stop, the upper part of his body kept going. He pitched forward over Corrigan to land with a crash on his hands and knees. He crouched there, dazed.

Corrigan jumped over to him. En route he glanced sidewise in time to see Chuck Baer finish with Charlie-the-Squeeze. The man-mountain was shaking what was left in his head; he had his hands up like a man groping in sudden darkness. Baer took the 360-pound muscleman by the nape with one hand and the crotch with the other, heaved, got him over his head, and threw him head-first at the wall. He landed on the floor in a foetal position, which was how he remained.

Corrigan grinned and completed the pacification of Tip Marks. The gunman was clawing under his sharkskin jacket. Corrigan kicked him in the belly. Marks let out a *whoosh!*, sat back against the wall, and threw up. Corrigan took a .38 out of Marks's shoulder holster, emptied its chambers, dropped the bullets into his pocket, and threw the pistol at Marks's face. Rather to his regret, it missed.

He straightened up and looked around. Not much time had passed—a few seconds. Charlie-the-Squeeze was lying near the wall on the other side of the bedroom, vastly out and bleeding at the scalp. The young blond giant, Hans, was peacefully asleep on the floor behind the rubbing table. Alfonze the Tip Marks was still producing the remains of his breakfast on the parquet floor.

He nodded, and he and Baer grinned at each other. The war was over.

Then he looked with his ungrinning eye at Herman Potts.

The bloated bookie had slid from the table; he was clutching the towel to his waist.

He said in a machine-gun voice, "I-didn't sic-'em-on-you-Captain-I-was-trying-to-stop-'em!"

Corrigan went slowly toward him.

"Honest, Captain! I never meant Hans to start nothing. They just went nuts all of a sudden, the three of 'em."

He stopped inches from Track-Odds. "You got it wrong, Herman, you know that? As I remember it, all four of you attacked us. And all four of you ended up on the floor. Isn't that how you remember it, Chuck?"

"Yes, sir," Baer said in an aggrieved voice. "Four against two peace officers. Fats here ended up in the hospital."

Potts's wattles began doing a dance; he back-pedaled with remarkable agility. "Now look, Officers, if I'm under arrest I ain't resisting!"

"Who said anything about arresting you, Herman?" Corrigan said, following him. "I'm just about to protect myself from your attack, and you'll probably yell police brutality. Well, I can't help that."

Potts had reached the wall; he tried to burrow into it and retain the modesty of his towel at the same time. "You can't hit me without I resist," he chattered, "and I ain't resisting, Captain! Look, I'm willing to cooperate."

"Oh," Corrigan said from a distance of three inches. "He's willing to cooperate, Chuck."

"I don't hear any cooperation, Tim," said Baer.

"About this Frank guy!" shouted Potts.

"Oh?" Corrigan said. "What about him, Herman?"

The bookie moistened his blubber-lips. "You won't collar me for booking bets, Captain?"

"What about him, I said!"

"Okay, okay," Potts said hastily. "Frank owes me this twenty-five thousand, see. No problem, though. He was coming up with it in a couple days. And that's the truth, Captain!"

"Coming up with it from where?"

Potts's fat shook in waves. "Where my customers get their scratch, I don't ask. It was the McCoy, though. I can always tell a stall from the real thing."

Corrigan glanced at Baer, who gave him the merest nod. So it sounded kosher to Chuck, too.

To Herman Potts, Corrigan said, "Did Frank give you any hint about where he was getting the money?"

"He just said he had a deal cooking and he'd pay me off by Friday at the latest. I wish I knew from where myself. I could maybe collect from his estate or something."

Corrigan was thinking. Finally he said, "Does the name Tony Turnboldt mean anything to you?"

The bookie shook his head.

"How about Sally Peterson? Wanda Hitchey?"

Potts shook his head again. "Who are they?"

On a hunch Corrigan decided to answer him. "Some people who work on the same floor of the Bower Building."

"Oh?" Potts said. He shook his head. "I don't know 'em. The only one I know on that floor besides Frank is a guy named Craft, Howie Craft."

As casually as he could, Corrigan said, "Howard Craft? How do you know Craft?"

Track-Odds looked unhappy. "You ain't setting me up for a bookmaking rap?"

"I told you no. Did Brian Frank introduce him to you?"

"No, no. Craft is another customer of mine. I mean was."

"Regular?"

"Well . . . yeah, you might say that."

"How's his luck been running?"

"Lousy. Worse even than Frank's."

"How lousy? How much did he drop to you, for instance, in the past twelve months?"

"Over fifty grand."

"Is he into you for it?"

"Oh, no. Craft's strictly a cash player. He pays off regular the end of every week."

Where would Howard Craft get that kind of money? Corrigan wondered. And what would old Everett Griswald think of his nephew's losing so much on the horses? Considering Brian Frank's propensity for blackmail, could his "deal" have been that he was shaking down Craft in return for silence about his gambling? He wouldn't be the first blackmailer to get paid off with a bullet.

Corrigan shook his head. Howard Craft had an iron alibi.

Just the same, he would have to check it through. "Did Brian Frank know about Howard Craft's losses, Herman?"

"Not from me he didn't," Potts said quickly. "I don't—didn't—run a canary business. Confidential service, like. I mean, it used to be."

"But Brian knew Craft was your client, too?" Corrigan persisted.

The fat man made a palms-up gesture. "Unless Craft told him. I never mentioned either one to the other."

And there went a possible motive to go along with the alibi.

Corrigan shrugged. "Let's get out of here, Chuck."

On the twenty-first floor of the Bower Building, Corrigan and Baer separated. Baer went up the hall to Burns Accounting, to report to his client. Corrigan turned into Griswald Jewelers. The door was open.

Old Everett Griswald was still at his desk. Corrigan loosened his topcoat and took a chair. The old jeweler looked up, irritated.

Corrigan managed to keep the dislike out of his voice. "I thought you'd close up, Mr. Griswald."

"My customers don't know about the vault," Griswald croaked. "Somebody has to be here to explain why we can't sell today."

Corrigan saw that he had been studying a copy of the audit report. "About your nephew," Corrigan said. "Is he well fixed financially?"

He could have sworn that the old ears pricked up. "Why?"

"During the last year Howie's dropped over fifty thousand dollars betting on horses. I wondered where he got it."

The old man looked astounded. "Impossible! You're mistaken."

"I got the information from the horse's mouth. Or the nearest thing to it. His bookmaker just told me."

Griswald's gray face turned bluish. He began quickly to fumble with the audit report he had been reading. Corrigan watched him. When the old jeweler reached the end of the report, he sat back with relief.

"He didn't embezzle it," he said. "Burns Accounting is a good outfit. Their audit would catch anything out of order. Besides, Howie didn't keep my books, Laverne did."

"Then where do you suppose he got the money, Mr. Griswald?"

"That bookmaker lied to you. Howie only makes a hundred a week take-home. And he's got nothing laid by. If I've told him a thousand times about being thrifty—"

Corrigan got to his feet. "How long will you be here, sir?"

"Till five. Howie and I will come back at nine tonight to open and reset the vault. The time-lock will release at ten after nine."

"Thank you, sir," Corrigan said; and he went up the hall to 2101. Chuck Baer was talking to Carleton Burns in the private office.

"Mr. Burns, you have the Griswald Jewelers books here, don't you?"

"I think they're still on Brian Frank's desk," Burns said. "Why, Captain?"

"And I assume you keep a copy of audit reports?"

"Of course. It would be on file."

"I wonder if you'd do me a favor."

Baer was beginning to look like a bloodhound that has just caught the scent.

Old Burns smiled. "Anything that's not illegal, Captain."

Corrigan did not smile back. He glanced over his shoulder, saw that the office door was open, went over, shut it carefully, and came back. He leaned over Carleton Burns's desk and spoke for some time in a low voice.

When he stopped, Burns looked thoughtful. At last the head of the accountancy firm nodded and glanced at his watch.

"I'd guess it will take a good four hours, Captain, and I'll have to break for dinner; I'm a diabetic, and I have to eat on time. Could you phone me about eight?"

"Will do," Corrigan said; and then he said, "Thank you," and nodded to Baer.

24.

They took the two girls to a steak haunt of Chuck Baer's. In the middle of their coffee Corrigan pushed his chair back, said, "Excuse me," and made for the restaurant's phone booth.

When he came back he was chewing his cud. Baer, who noticed everything, said, "Okay?"

"I guess." But Corrigan sounded dissatisfied. "It was pretty much as I'd figured. Only it makes no sense."

"I don't like you when you're grim," Sybil said. "Wasn't that the phone call you said you couldn't make till eight?"

"I did," Corrigan said, glancing at his watch for the tenth time. "It's five after."

Sybil showed him hers. "You're caught, Captain. It's only five minutes to eight by a watch that keeps perfect time."

This time Corrigan looked unbelieving. "I'm a bug on timepieces. This thing set me back two hundred dollars. You're wrong, Sybil."

"She's right," Baer said, and turned to Sally Peterson. "What does your watch show, baby?"

Corrigan stared down at the three wrists. They all said 7:55.

"Bingo," he said.

"What?" said Baer.

"That's how it was done!"

"I need one last piece," Corrigan said rapidly. His chair scraped back. "Look, I'm sorry, but we're going to have to call tonight's socializing off. I've got to go back to work."

"You've figured it," Baer said slowly. He rose, too. "I want in, Tim. Is it okay for the girls—"

"I'm still one of Tim's suspects," Sybil said. Her blue eyes were expectant.

"You haven't been a suspect of mine for a long time, Sybil." A long time. . . . When did night fall? It seemed a century ago. Time had a way of stretching itself, like a rubber band.

"How about me?" asked Sally Peterson in her usual mocking tone.

Corrigan did not look at her. "Oh, you're invited, too, Sally," he said casually, and asked, "Will the Bower Building be locked now?"

"It's never locked. They post a man in the lobby at nine o'clock and all you have to do is sign in and out."

"Then let's go," Corrigan said.

It was a quarter of nine when the foursome stepped off on the twenty-first floor. The floor was negotiable in the night light, but all three offices were dark and, as Corrigan quickly determined, locked.

"What are we doing here?" Sybil asked. "Nobody's here."

The grim look on Corrigan's face was deeper. "Somebody will be. Sally, do you happen to have a key to the Adams office?"

The blonde nodded. "I also know where Tony hid the happy juice left over from last night."

"Great," Chuck Baer said; he was watching Corrigan closely. "Nothing I like better than a slug or two when I'm waiting for a payoff. How long do you figure, Tim?"

"Ten, fifteen minutes," Corrigan said.

But when Sally unlocked the door to the Adams Advertising Agency and let them into the reception office, it developed that no one wanted a drink without ice, not even Baer. They dumped their wraps and settled for a smoke in the semidarkness of a night light. Sally Peterson and the redheaded detective sprawled, not touching, on the sofa. Sybil perched on the edge of Eva Benson's desk chair. Corrigan had the door to the hall open a few inches; his eye remained trained on the elevator.

At three minutes past nine the elevator door opened. Old Everett Griswald bustled out, followed by his nephew.

Corrigan motioned. "Here we go."

The old jeweler was in the act of unlocking the door to 2102 when the four descended on him and Howard Craft.

"Captain Corrigan," Craft said. He stared in amazement at the two girls.

Corrigan said, "We stopped by to witness the opening of the safe. Or, rather, I did; Baer and the

231

girls happen to be with me. Do you mind?"

Old Griswald pocketed the key, looking at Corrigan. "What is it, Captain? You think something's going to turn up missing?"

Corrigan smiled and shook his head. "I'm pretty sure everything locked in yesterday is still there, Mr. Griswald. It's a routine part of my investigation. We have to check everything out, you know."

With a shrug the old man pushed open the door and switched on the overhead light.

He led the way into his private office. He turned on the light and hung his coat and hat on the clothestree. Howard Craft unbuttoned his coat; he kept it on.

Everett Griswald glanced at the wall clock. It showed six minutes past nine. "You figure four minutes yet, Howie?"

"I told you, Uncle Everett. I set it at five P.M. for sixteen hours. The blackout lasted twelve hours and ten minutes. So it should open at nine-ten."

They presented a tableau. For four minutes nobody changed position. In a curious way, the silence thickened. Old Griswald began to look from face to face in a worried way. Howie Craft took out a cigaret, looked at it, then seemed to forget about it. It remained in his fingers, unlit.

At exactly ten past nine the old jeweler tried the vault door. He tugged and tugged. It failed to open. He waited a full minute and tried again. Again it failed to open.

He frowned at his nephew. "You're sure about the timeset, Howie?"

"I don't understand it," Craft said nervously.

"The power going off suddenly must have loused it up some way."

In a conversational tone Corrigan remarked, "It'll open in a few minutes. My guess is around twenty after."

If the silence had been thick before, it was positively solid now. Old Griswald's gray nostrils were fluttering as if to test the wind; there was something curiously like panic in his veined and swimming eyes. Howard Craft stood perfectly still, the picture of a men's-store dummy. His thin face was almost as gray as his uncle's. It was as if he felt a blow coming, but from which direction he was unsure. He had his neat little eyes fixed on the vault door.

At nine-fifteen the old man tried the door. It was still locked.

At nine-sixteen he tried again. Still locked.

At nine-seventeen. Eighteen. Nineteen. Twenty . . .

It opened.

"Hold it, Mr. Griswald," Corrigan said, and stepped over to the vault. Baer was just behind him. They studied the three dials on the inside of the massive door. One set the time by number of hours expired, one the number of minutes to sixty; the third was a clock face.

Instead of registering 9:20, as the wall clock did, the vault clock registered 9:10.

"That blackout was a bad break, Craft," Corrigan said, and turned around. Craft seemed paralyzed. "You were always first in the office. You could have reset the vault clock to the right time this morning before your uncle got in, if it hadn't been for the power failure, and nobody would ever have known the difference. The evidence would have been wiped out."

"Evidence," Howard Craft said from still lips. "I don't know—I can't imagine—what you're talking about."

"How you choose to plead, my friend, is a matter for the district attorney's office and your lawyer, not me." He moved casually, and somewhere he was between Craft and the door. Craft stood there trying to get some moisture on his lips. "Chuck, you happen to recall Laverne Thomas's glancing at that miniature watch of hers, then saying how long the power'd been off?"

"I have total recall about some things," Baer said with a straight face. The man in the sharply pressed suit would have been comical in other circumstances. "I remember Laverne's exact words: 'Seven thirty-five, which means the power's already been off two hours and twenty-seven minutes.' I'm pulling your leg. I have a lousy memory. But the reason I remember what Laverne said is that I thought at the time she wasn't very good at figuring, and she a bookkeeper. She'd made a mistake by ten minutes. Now I realize—"

"—that her figuring was right; it was her data that were wrong," Corrigan nodded. "Which has to mean that she thought the power failure had come at five-o-eight instead of at five-eighteen."

He turned to Craft again. "What Laverne Thomas actually remembered when she phoned me last night to say she knew Brian Frank's killer,

Craft, was that the clock in your uncle's office here and the one in the display room out there had registered five-eight when the electricity went off, but since that time had somehow—both clocks—jumped ahead ten minutes. It told her the whole story, as it's now told us. You couldn't reset the clock in the vault, of course, because you couldn't get at it."

Everett Griswald was gaping like a carp out of water. "What is all this, Captain Corrigan?" he gulped. "I don't follow any of it! You mean Howard—"

"I mean Howard," Corrigan nodded. "Mr. Griswald, you'd better get set for some more bad news. When you recheck your inventory it's my considered opinion you'll find around one hundred thousand dollars' worth of your jewelry missing."

The gape turned to a gasp; the gray took on a lovely blue tinge. The old eyes watered in his nephew's direction. Howie Craft seemed to be dwindling on the spot, like Alice in the Shrink-Me phase of her adventures.

"I mean, that's what undoubtedly financed your nephew Howard's horse-betting losses, Mr. Griswald. I put it at one hundred grand's worth of jewelry taken because he could hardly have fenced them for more than fifty percent."

"But it can't be," the old man said in a cracked whisper. "The audit . . . Laverne kept my books . . ."

"Miss Thomas didn't take inventory," Corrigan said. "Mr. Howard Craft did that. So the inventory figures entered in Miss Thomas's books are merely what Howie told her they should be. But Burns Accounting makes its own inventories when it audits. So Brian Frank discovered the embezzlement. It turned out that Frank was a practicing blackmailer. Instead of revealing the shortage, he took your nephew aside and agreed to cover it up if Howie would steal even more from you and pay him twenty-five thousand dollars to retire his own gambling debt."

Howard Craft was looking at Corrigan as if the MOS man were a mind-reader.

"Your company books, Mr. Griswald, are still in the possession of Burns Accounting. I had Mr. Burns recheck them tonight. In Brian Frank's desk he found a record of the true inventory Frank had made, and it didn't agree at all with either Laverne Thomas's ledger entries or the audit report Frank turned in."

Sally Peterson suddenly said, "What about his alibi, Captain?"

"I thought I had explained that."

Sally said, "Not to my satisfaction. I didn't follow it clearly. I suppose I'm dumb."

"Then I am, too," Sybil confessed. "I've been ashamed to ask for clarification."

"All right," Corrigan smiled, "I'll spell it out. When Craft returned to this office after leaving Brian Frank up the hall he set back both wall clocks here and the vault mechanism ten minutes. Then he took the P38 from his uncle's desk, climbed out the window there, and worked his way along the ledge to Frank's office." He looked at

Craft. "Frank could hardly have missed hearing you. I suppose when you pushed up his window you covered him with the pistol and told him to stay put."

The old jeweler's nephew, like his uncle, seemed incapable of speech.

"You shot him, and promptly worked your way back along the ledge. By then it must actually have been about seven after five, but the clocks you'd monkeyed with here registered only four fifty-seven. You ran across the display room, stuck your head in Laverne's office, and told her it was time to set the vault. There's no clock in her office, and her watch face was so tiny she had to strain to see it. So she must simply have accepted the time the wall clocks registered. Why should she think that both clocks and the one in the vault were wrong? So you had your alibi, and Laverne didn't see through it till the middle of the night, in the blackout."

Sybil said in a horrified voice, "He murdered Laverne, too!"

"He sure did, Irish," Corrigan said. "He was bedded down in his uncle's office here. He listened in on her phone call to me over the extension there on Mr. Griswald's desk, realized she was going to finger him, ran into her office, and shut her mouth for good. He was back in here pretending to be asleep before I got my shoes on."

Old Griswald seemed to awaken from the dream world he had been inhabiting for the past few minutes. Before either Corrigan or Baer could stop him, he was dancing before his nephew in a rage, grabbing the petrified clerk by the immaculate lapels, shaking him like a child.

"Stupid! Dumbhead!" the old jeweler shrieked. "Did you have to steal from yourself? Who else do I have to leave it to? Now I'll have to give it all to charity!"

Chuck Baer stepped between them, grasped the livid old man by the elbows, lifted him gently, and stood him to one side.

"You can think that one over, Howie," Baer said, "while you're paying the tab for your two kills. Personally, I don't think this miser's dough could go for a better cause—no matter what the hell the cause is. Shall we go, Captain Corrigan?"

"Not without Mr. Craft," said Captain Corrigan. "I'm sorry girls, I'll have to let Chuck take you home. Maybe there'll be another blackout tomorrow night. Tonight Mr. Craft and I are going to be tied up."